Undo the handcuffs now, boys," Mom said in that calm controlled voice.

"You did it!" I said to my little brother. He nodded.

"Great, let's go."

"Wait!" Mom called.

Benjy stopped. I grabbed his hand and pulled.

"Steven, Benjamin, where are you going?" Mom demanded. "You can't leave me like this."

I shoved Benjy through the front door and turned back to her. "We'll be back, Mom. We just want you to get used to it."

"Used to what?" Mom asked.

"Being our prisoner."

Also by Todd Strasser

Kidnap Kids

Todd Strasser

Penguin Putnam Books for Young Readers

A PaperStar Book, published in 1999 by
Penguin Putnam Books for Young Readers,
345 Hudson Street, New York, NY 10014.
PaperStar is a registered trademark of The Putnam Berkley Group, Inc.
The PaperStar logo is a trademark of The Putnam Berkley Group, Inc.
Originally published in 1998 by G. P. Putnam's Sons.
Published simultaneously in Canada.
Printed in the United States of America.
Book design by Gary Bernal. Text set in Sabon.
Library of Congress Cataloging-in-Publication Data
Strasser, Todd. Kidnap kids / Todd Strasser. p. cm.
Summary: Twelve-year-old Steven and his younger brother Benjy
make a desperate attempt to force their extremely busy parents
to spend more time together with them. [1. Parent and child—Fiction.
2. Family life—Fiction.] I. Title. PZ7.S899Ki 1998 [Fic]—dc21
97-36301 CIP AC ISBN 0-698-11801-4
3 5 7 9 10 8 6 4

This story is based on an idea from my friend and fishing buddy Steven Roberts. It is dedicated to his children: Sam, Charlie, and Lily.

Introduction

This is the story of how my nine-year-old brother, Benjy, and I kidnapped our parents. But don't get the wrong idea. This *isn't* a How-to book or anything like that. Let's face it, the *last* thing most kids want to do is kidnap their own parents. In fact, most kids I know wish their parents would get kidnapped by someone else and disappear forever.

However, if you read this book you'll see that things were pretty bad for Benjy and me. We weren't allowed to see our friends, and we hardly ever got anything fun to eat. Given our situation, I think you'll understand why we had to take drastic action.

"You sweating, Steven?" Benjy whispered.

"No," I whispered back. We were hiding in my closet. The door was open just enough for us to see out.

"You *sure?*" he asked.

"I think I'd *know* if I was sweating. Now be quiet."

"Boys?" Sonja called from the hall outside my room. Sonja was our nanny. She had short blond hair, big teeth, and spoke with an accent.

"It is past bedtime, boys," Sonja said.

We didn't answer her.

"Do not be like this." Sonja pushed on the door. Balanced on top of it was a plastic bucket filled with ice water.

The bucket tipped.

Ker-splash!

It landed upside down on Sonja's head. The water settled into the carpet around her feet, leaving a big dark puddle. Ice cubes glimmered on the surface of the puddle like jewels.

Sonja yanked off the bucket and tucked it under her arm. Her hair was plastered to her head. Her eyes got squinty, and the corners of her mouth turned down. She grumbled angrily in her language and ran up the stairs to her room on the third floor.

I pushed open the closet door.

"Think she's gonna quit?" Benjy asked as he followed me out. He has blond hair and blue eyes, which is weird because I have dark-brown hair and brown eyes.

"They usually do," I answered.

From downstairs came the squeak of the front door as Mom let herself into our town house. *Bleep!* She reactivated the alarm and bolted the door shut behind her. It was 10:45 at night. Most moms would be going to bed. Ours was just getting home from work.

Her shoes tapped up the stairs. A moment later she stopped in the doorway to my room. Mom has dark-brown hair and brown eyes like me. She's not very big. Barefoot, she's the same height as me and weighs only about five pounds more. I'm twelve and a half.

She was wearing a dark-blue dress. In one hand was

a brown leather briefcase. Over the other shoulder was a large black leather bag stuffed with legal documents. She always brought work home.

"What happened?" She looked down at the puddle on the floor. "Where's Sonja? Why is there water on the floor? What are you doing up at this hour?"

"A bucket of water fell on Sonja's head," Benjy reported solemnly.

Mom's mouth fell open. "A buck— Oh, no, you didn't!"

The thumping sound of feet came down the stairs from the third floor, accompanied by muffled banging. Sonja was dragging a big gray suitcase down to the second-floor landing.

She had changed into dry clothes but her hair was still soaked. She started down the stairs to the first floor.

"Sonja?" Mom called after her. "Sonja, wait!"

The suitcase thumped down the stairs to the first floor. Sonja wasn't waiting for anyone.

"Sonja, please!" Mom dropped her bag and briefcase and hurried down the stairs behind her.

Benjy and I went out to the second-floor landing and watched from the railing. Sonja stopped in the front hall near the door. She jabbed the keypad on the wall with her finger, trying to deactivate the alarm system. Mom stood close by with her arms crossed. She spoke in that low, controlled voice she used whenever life threatened to reach critical mass.

"I am truly sorry for what they did and I will see that they are punished . . . severely," Mom said. "But, Sonja, you can't leave. I'm in the middle of an unbelievably important trial. It concerns national security. I'm sure you've seen it on TV."

Above the keypad a small red light blinked on and off. Sonja had messed up the deactivation code. She muttered to herself and started over.

"Sonja, please, listen," Mom begged. "I have work to do tonight. I have to be back in court early tomorrow morning. My husband's somewhere in Asia. There's no one to take care of the boys."

Sonja kept jabbing the keypad.

"Suppose I told you the president of the United States himself called today about the trial?" Mom asked, then waited to see what impact that would have.

Up on the second-floor landing, Benjy looked at me and whispered, "Serious?"

I shrugged. Sometimes Mom said things that weren't exactly true. Meanwhile Sonja kept jabbing the keypad and muttering to herself. She didn't buy the presidential stuff.

4

Mom tried a different approach. "Maybe you'd like a raise?"

Sonja made a fist and hit the keypad. *Thunk!*

"How about a hundred dollars a week more than you're getting now?" Mom offered. "And as soon as the trial is over we'll give you a two-week vacation . . . with pay."

Sonja turned to the door and slid the bolt open.

"Don't!" Mom gasped.

Too late. Sonja yanked open the door.

The alarm made a screeching high-pitched whine. Benjy and I stuck our fingers in our ears.

Groof! Groof! Pearson, our big yellow Labrador retriever, bounded out of the kitchen, barking like crazy. Mom quickly punched the deactivation code on the keypad.

By the time the racket stopped, Sonja had dragged her suitcase outside and vanished into the dark. Mom would have followed her, but a police officer appeared in the doorway.

Groof! Pearson tried to jump on the police officer, but Mom grabbed his collar.

"Pearson! Down!" She struggled to hold our dog back, but Pearson was too strong. Even with his paws sliding on the hardwood floor, he started to drag her toward the officer.

"Boys!" Mom yelled up to us. "Call Pearson."

"Up here, Pearson," Benjy called. The dog turned and climbed the stairs with his tongue hanging out and his tail wagging. He sat down next to us on the second-floor landing and licked Benjy's ear. Benjy put his arms around Pearson's neck and hugged him.

"Everything okay, Mrs. Marks?" The police officer peered over Mom's head at Benjy and me. We waved back.

"Yes. I'm sorry," Mom apologized. "It was just an accident."

The officer unclipped a black walkie-talkie from his belt and spoke into it. "False alarm . . . Yeah . . . Okay . . ." He held the walkie-talkie toward Mom. "It's Lieutenant Carson."

Mom rolled her eyes and looked annoyed. "I told you it was just an accident."

"Sorry, ma'am, it's procedure." The police officer handed her the walkie-talkie.

Mom pressed it to her ear. "Yes? . . . Well, I'm sorry, but these things happen . . . I have two young boys who don't understand that . . . No, I will not . . . Because I don't want to frighten them . . ."

"Ahem," the police officer cleared his throat to get Mom's attention, then glanced up at Benjy and me. Mom's eyes darted toward us, and I could see that she didn't want us to hear. She and the officer went outside, leaving the door slightly ajar behind them.

Benjy turned to me. "Frightened of what, Steven?"

"The Nut Bombers, I guess."

"I thought they were in jail."

I nodded and didn't answer. It didn't totally make sense to me either.

A few moments later Mom came back in, locked the door, and reactivated the alarm. Benjy and I were still sitting behind the rail on the second-floor landing. She looked up at us. The skin under her eyes looked dark and saggy. A few thick strands of hair fell down on her forehead. One side of her skirt was covered with Pearson's white hair.

"Why?" she asked. We knew she was talking about Sonja.

"The Oreo chunks were always soggy," answered Benjy, who had to have Oreo pancakes every morning at breakfast.

Mom blinked with astonishment. "You poured a bucket of water on her head because she made soggy pancakes?"

"She wasn't nice to us," I said.

Mom shook her head wearily. "Five months, five nannies." She checked her watch. "Eleven o'clock

at night and I have no one to take care of you tomorrow."

"Did the president really call?" Benjy asked.

"One of his advisors spoke to Jack," Mom replied.
Jack was Mom's boss. He was the one who'd assigned
her to prosecute the Nut Bombers. The TV said Mom
was the state's star prosecutor.

"Then why'd you tell Sonja the president called?"
Benjy wanted to know.

"I said *suppose* the president had called," Mom explained. "I was trying to make her understand the im-
portance of this case."

"Isn't that lying?" Benjy asked.

Mom shook her head. "No. An exaggeration, maybe.
But not a lie." Because she was a lawyer, Mom was really careful about what she said.

She took a small gray electronic organizer out of
her jacket pocket and started pressing the keys on the
little keyboard. From another pocket she took out a
black cell phone and punched in a number. She pressed
the phone to her ear. "Mrs. Woburn? It's Megan
Marks. I'm sorry to bother you so late . . . Yes, I'm
afraid so. She just walked out . . . No, I don't know
why she left . . . Well, I have to have someone here in
the morning . . . Yes, I understand that, but you must
have *someone* . . . Please, Mrs. Woburn, it's late and

I'm very tired. I don't need this lecture now . . . What? Where am I going to find another service at this time of night? . . . How can you say that?"

Mom yanked the cell phone away from her ear and punched a button. The phone went dead.

"How come you said you didn't know why Sonja left?" Benjy asked.

"What would you like me to say?" Mom asked back. "That you dumped a bucket of water on her head?"

Benjy and I shared a grin.

Mom pressed her fingers against the sides of her forehead. "It's late, boys. I have a lot to do. Please, go to bed."

"Can I sleep in Steven's room?" Benjy asked.

"No."

"*Please?*" Benjy begged.

"Oh, okay, just go to bed."

We went into my room. The truth was, Benjy stayed with me almost every night. The floor had carpet, and Benjy usually slept between two thick feather comforters. He used this big brown stuffed bear named Puffy as a pillow. Most nights Pearson shared Puffy Bear with him.

I got into bed, and Benjy slid between the comforters on the floor. We were supposed to wash our faces and brush our teeth, but we hardly ever did. Mom and Dad were usually too busy to check, and the nannies didn't care. I sometimes rinsed with mouthwash in the morning so I wouldn't have mutant breath at school.

"If the Nut Bombers are in jail, how come the police are outside our house?" Benjy asked after I read him a story about a boy who switched bodies with his dog.

"I think there might be other members of their group around," I said.

Benjy yawned. "What would they want with us?"

"I don't know, Benjy."

"Hey, now! Rise and shine!" a voice ordered the next morning. I opened my eyes. Standing in the middle of the room was Dewey Van DeHey. Dewey was thin and not much taller than me even though he was a lot older. He had cool tattoos of mermaids and daggers and snakes on his arms, and he always wore a black T-shirt with the sleeves rolled up so you could see them. He was wearing baggy green pants with lots of big pockets, and black boots. His blond hair was crew cut, and he had gold hoops in both ears and through one eyebrow.

"What are you doing here?" I asked, rubbing my eyes.

"Providing high-quality in-home security at an affordable rate," Dewey announced.

"Where's Mom?" asked Benjy from the floor.

"Gone to the trenches, rug rat," Dewey said.

Sometimes it was a little hard to figure out what Dewey was talking about. His family lived up the street in a town house twice the size of ours. Dewey had a bunch of brothers and sisters who'd all grown up and gone off to college. He was the only one left. I didn't exactly know his age, only that he didn't work or go to school. Dad sometimes paid him to play catch with Benjy.

"I've got my orders," Dewey announced. "First, get you two assembled for school." He went over to my closet and pulled out my blue blazer. "Feeling GQ, Benjo?" he asked my brother.

"That's mine," I said. "Benjy's clothes are in his room."

Dewey looked at the blazer. "Yeah, thought it looked a little large." He went to the door. "Accompany me, Private Benjamin."

Benjy untangled himself from the comforters and dragged Puffy Bear out of my room. I got out of bed and went to the bathroom. I was in the middle of gargling with mouthwash when I heard banging and thumping coming from my brother's room.

"Two points!" Dewey shouted.

"You fouled me!" Benjy yelled.

"Did not!" Dewey replied. "Gimmie that!"

I went into Benjy's room. The walls were covered with posters of baseball players. A couple of little-league trophies stood on top of Benjy's dresser, along with his mitt, rosin bag, and a hard ball. Benjy was curled up on the floor, his arms tucked tightly around a miniature basketball. Dewey was straddling him, trying to get the ball loose.

"It's mine!" Benjy wailed.

"Give it up, Furtart," Dewey grunted. "There are no fouls in bedroom basketball." He tore the ball out of Benjy's hands and slam-dunked the miniature plastic hoop over the doorway so hard the rim snapped off. Dewey bent down and picked up the broken piece.

"Inferior materials." He tossed the rim away.

"Way to go, Dewey." Benjy sniffed. He reached for his jeans. "Think I could have some privacy?"

"Whoa, is that what you call appreciation?" Dewey put his hands on his hips and pretended to be hurt. "I get up in the middle of the night to come over and break your basketball hoop, and all you can do is ask me to leave? Fine."

He went downstairs.

Benjy pulled on his pants, then said in a low voice, "He's not really gonna take care of us, is he?"

"Maybe for today," I whispered back. "Until Mom finds a new nanny."

I went back to my room and finished getting dressed. By the time I got downstairs, Benjy was slumped at the kitchen table with his hair sticking up. His sweater was inside out. The tag showed.

Dewey was sitting with his boots on the table, going through a stack of mail. "Whoa, chick pods, your parents are sixty days behind on the electric bill. They're gonna get nailed big time."

"You're not supposed to read our mail, Dewey," I said as I pulled open the refrigerator door.

"And anyway, they're not gonna get nailed," Benjy added. "My mom's the one who *does* the nailing."

I looked in the refrigerator. Except for some moldy-looking bread, a few bruised apples, and a plastic container of leftover SpaghettiOs, it looked pretty bare.

"Can I have chocolate milk?" Benjy asked.

"No milk," I said.

"Then I have to have ice cream," Benjy decided. "Dr. Sax says I have to have three glasses of milk a day if I want to play major-league ball. He said ice cream is okay if there's no milk."

"Sounds like my kind of doctor." Dewey grinned.

I took two bowls out of the kitchen cabinet. Dewey gave me a hungry look, so I got a third bowl. I took the cookies 'n' cream out of the freezer and brought it over to the kitchen table.

"What about the sprinkles?" Benjy asked.

"Get 'em yourself," I said.

Benjy moaned and groaned about getting up, but

he managed to find the red hot sprinkles and dump them on his ice cream.

"Have some ice cream with your sprinkles." I smirked.

"What about me, Piggo?" asked Dewey.

"Here." Benjy scooped a spoonful of sprinkles out of his bowl and dumped them on Dewey's ice cream.

"Thanks, Furtart," Dewey nodded.

"What's a Furtart?" Benjy asked.

"A Pop-Tart with fur, what else?" Dewey replied as if it were totally obvious.

Benjy and I shared a look of disbelief. Dewey was definitely bizarre.

Benjy ate only half of his ice cream. Dewey finished it for him. When it was time to go to school, I deactivated the alarm and Benjy and I went outside. Mr. Sam was down at the curb, talking with one of the policemen who sat in a patrol car outside our house each night. Mr. Sam had short brown hair and always wore aviator sunglasses so we couldn't see his eyes.

Benjy and I used to walk to school. After school we used to fool around with our friends and do stuff outside. But a few weeks ago things changed. We couldn't go to our friends' houses anymore, and Mom hired Mr. Sam to drive us to and from school. He must not have had much else to do because most of the time he just sat in his car across from the school all day, waiting for us.

"Ready for school, boys?" Mr. Sam asked the same thing every morning.

"No," Benjy and I always answered.

"That's the spirit." Mr. Sam held the back door of his car open, and we got in.

"Which way are we going today?" I asked. Mr. Sam had about six different routes for taking us to school. We never knew which way he was going to go.

"I thought I'd head down past the park," he said.

"How come you go so many different ways?" Benjy asked.

"It gets pretty boring if you always go the same way," Mr. Sam said. "So I like to mix it up."

Benjy gave me a look. I knew what he was thinking. Something about the Nut Bomber case had changed. And ever since then it had become impossible to find a grown-up who'd tell us the truth.

4

Dewey returned the next day and the day after that. During that time we never actually *saw* Mom in person. She was gone when we woke up, and didn't get back until after we were asleep. The only way we knew she'd actually been home were the notes she left for us each day on the kitchen table.

On the fourth morning Dewey arrived with a box of donut holes and the newspaper. Benjy sat at the kitchen table with his chin propped on his hands. His hair was a mess, and he was wearing the same wrinkled clothes he'd worn the previous two days. He'd slept in them. We'd been up past eleven for the last two nights.

Dewey put the box of donut holes in the middle of the kitchen table and opened it. He reached in and took out a handful. Then he opened the newspaper to the cartoons.

"Have some munchies, Benjo," he said as he popped three in his mouth at once.

"I don't like the ones with jelly in them," Benjy grumbled.

"Then eat the others," I said.

Benjy shook his head. "They've got white stuff on them."

"It's just powdered sugar," I said.

"I don't like it," Benjy whined. "Why can't I have Oreo pancakes?"

I looked at Dewey, who was busy reading the cartoons. His cheek bulged with donut holes, and his lower lip had a big smudge of white powdered sugar on it. It didn't seem likely that he'd know how to make Oreo pancakes.

I dug through the box until I found a couple of chocolate-glazed donut holes that didn't have much powdered sugar on them. I put them in front of Benjy, who picked one up and inspected it carefully. Then he popped it in his mouth.

Briiiing! The living room phone rang.

"Bet it's Mom!" Benjy jumped out of his chair and raced into the living room. Whenever Mom or Dad called, he had to talk to them first. I waited until he was finished.

• • •

"Hi, hon, how's it going?" Mom asked when it was my turn.

"Okay. How about you?"

"It's very busy," she said. "And I'm afraid it's going to get worse. We're entering the home stretch."

"When will we get to see you?" I asked.

I guess I caught her off guard because for a second she didn't know what to say. "I know, I've been a terrible mother. I promise we'll be together this weekend."

"That's not till the day after tomorrow," I said. "We used to see you in the morning and at night. Now it's like you don't even live here."

"You can always catch me on the news," she said.

It was my turn not to know what to say.

Mom cleared her throat. "That was supposed to be a joke, hon."

"Oh."

"I guess it wasn't very funny," she admitted.

"I know it's a really important trial, Mom," I said. "But Dad's away and you're never around and it's like we don't even have parents anymore."

"That's not true," Mom said.

"Well, that's what it *feels* like," I said.

"Steven, honey, this trial can't last another month," she said. "Once it's over I'm going to take a nice long vacation and spend it with you and Benjy."

"When this trial's over there'll probably be another one," I said.

"No, hon, not like this," Mom insisted.

"Even when there isn't a trial you work all the time," I said.

"It's going to be different."

"Yeah, right." I didn't believe her.

"I promised Benjy I'd get that video game this weekend." Mom tried to change the subject. "The racing car one."

"Nice try, Mom." I glanced over at the kitchen counter, where Dewey was pouring big glasses of Coke for himself and Benjy. Then I stretched the telephone cord into the living room and spoke in a low voice. "Who's going to take care of us?"

"Do you like Dewey?" Mom asked.

"Are you serious?" I asked back.

"What's the point of getting another nanny if you're just going to dump a bucket of water on her head?"

"How do you know we won't do that to Dewey?" I asked.

"Because I think you like him."

She was right. We did like Dewey. Probably because

he let us stay up late and eat whatever we wanted. But inside I knew it wasn't supposed to be that way.

"Hon, I have to go into a meeting," Mom said, her voice rushed. "I'll see you tonight."

"I'll be asleep," I said.

"We'll have all weekend together. Gotta go. I love you." She hung up.

I put the phone down and went back to the kitchen. At the kitchen table Dewey gulped down his glass of Coke and then let out a burp. Benjy took a gulp of *his* Coke and burped right back. Dewey grinned, swallowed some air, and belched even louder. Meanwhile Pearson had his paws up on the table and managed to snag an unclaimed donut hole.

Dewey take care of us?

Talk about the nuts taking over the nuthouse.

Mom and Dad weren't always this busy. When I was younger, Dad and I used to play catch and shoot baskets in the school yard. Mom taught me to ride a bike, and we used to go on rides (Benjy's nine and he still hasn't learned to ride). They took us to shows and the circus and Sunday brunch.

But then they got busier and busier until their idea of spending time with us was taking us to the store to buy a new game so we'd have something to do while they worked.

On Saturday morning Mom bought us Dual Quantum U-Race, this awesome cool racing video game. It came with two steering wheels and gearshifts, and a choice of about fifty different video racetracks and terrains.

Benjy and I raced each other all weekend. Mom

spent most of the time on the phone or working on her laptop computer.

On Sunday night we went out for dinner, then hurried home to wait for Dad to call. He's the director of technical services for a company that's been laying a fiber-optic cable from Tokyo to London.

Dad said the fiber-optic cable was only an inch and a half thick, but it could carry 10,000 times more information (mostly telephone calls) than the copper cable it was replacing. Most of it was submarine cable, meaning it went underwater, but Dad was in the process of laying about 100 miles of it through jungles across the Malay Peninsula.

The living room phone rang and it was Dad on his satellite telephone, sounding like he was two blocks away instead of in Penang, Malaysia. When Dad asked how things were, Mom said everything was great. She'd warned us ahead of time not to say anything about Sonja leaving because Dad already had enough to worry about.

We asked when he'd be home.

In a week, he said.

Later Mom read to Benjy until he fell asleep, then went into her room. I waited a little while, then got out of bed and knocked on her door. I expected to find her going through papers or talking on the phone. Instead she was standing in front of the wall mirror, wearing a green dress with tags hanging from it.

"What do you think?" she asked.

"Looks nice," I said.

"Holly Roberts told me I had to get some new clothes."

"Who?"

"The court reporter for *The News*," Mom explained. "She overheard some TV people complaining that I always wear the same old clothes and I look frumpy. Do *you* think I look frumpy?"

"I don't even know what it means," I said.

"It means old and wrinkled. Too school-marmish."

"So?"

"It's bad for ratings or something," Mom said, still studying herself in the mirror. "The audience wants to see me in something new."

"What audience?"

"The people who watch the trial coverage on TV," Mom said. "I know it's stupid. What I wear should have nothing to do with the trial. But I worry about the jury. There are subliminal factors."

"What's that?"

"Impressions you make on people," Mom explained. "Things they may not even be aware of that could affect their decisions."

"You mean they might decide to let the Nut

Bombers go because you wore the same old clothes?"

Mom gave me a wan smile. "When you put it that way it sounds pretty dumb, doesn't it?"

I nodded.

"But you don't want to take any chances," Mom went on. "It's such a hard trial. These militia people are incredibly dangerous, and we want them to go to jail for a long time. The problem is they never actually blew anything up."

"But they had all the explosives and stuff," I said. "And you have the tapes of them making plans."

"Yes," said Mom. "But can you convince the jury that these people should be severely punished for simply *planning* to blow up buildings? How do you prove that they were really serious and not just trying to impress each other? People make plans and break them all the time."

"I'll say."

Mom stared at me, then lowered her eyes. "That's not fair, Steven."

"I didn't mean it that way," I said. I wasn't even thinking about our family, although you'd need a supercomputer to count the number of times my parents had planned vacations only to cancel them at the last minute because of work. Not that it had *always* been that way. Just the past year or two.

"Anyway, that's all going to change after the trial,"

26

Mom said, and looked back at the mirror. "I don't know. Maybe it's the shoes."

I looked at her shoes. They were black and shiny. The heels were narrower and higher than the shoes she normally wore.

"I thought a higher heel would help me look taller and more commanding," she said. "Or are they too suggestive?"

"What's that?" I asked.

Mom shook her head. "It's not important, hon. I shouldn't be bothering you with this." She turned to the mirror again.

"Mom, I'm worried about Benjy," I said.

Mom looked at me in the mirror. The lines between her eyebrows sloped into a deep V. "Why?"

"I don't think this is good for him," I said. "I mean, you and Dad being gone so much."

Mom's shoulders sagged. She turned away from the mirror, kicked off the new shoes, and plopped down onto the bed beside me. She put her arm around my shoulders. "I don't know what to say. I wish I could be in two places at once, but I can't."

"There's stuff you don't know about," I said. "Like all the junk we eat and how late we stay up. And his teeth, Mom. I don't think he's brushed them in *months*."

"Oh, come on." She thought I was exaggerating.

27

"I'm *serious*," I insisted.

Mom took a long deep breath. "I'm glad we're talking, Steven. It must be hard for you to understand why I'm not home more. You must think I'm in control of my life, that I could spend more time at home if I really wanted to. What if I told you I'm not in control of my own life?"

"Why not?"

She raised her hands in a helpless gesture and let them fall into her lap. "Because of this case. The people of this city . . . *the whole country* . . . are counting on me to put these guys away. Lord knows I want this trial to end as soon as possible. But it has to end with a conviction. I have a moral and ethical obligation."

"Why can't you hand it over to someone else?" I asked.

"Because I'm the lead prosecutor," she said. "The jury wouldn't understand it if I left. They'd think there was an internal conflict. They'd interpret it as a sign of weakness in our case."

"Couldn't you just say you needed to spend more time with your kids?" I asked.

Mom looked me straight in the eye. "Steven, I love you and Benjy more than anything in the world. There is nothing I wouldn't do for you. And if you want to know the truth, I think taking this case was a mistake.

But I agreed to do it and now I have to stay with it until the end. It's too late change."

I nodded, but it still bothered me. There were kids I knew whose parents weren't around because there'd been a divorce, or one of them had died. But I was the only kid I knew who had parents who were too busy to be parents.

Mom looked at her watch. "It's late, hon. You better go to bed." She kissed me on the forehead.

I got up and started out, but stopped in the doorway. "Why do we need the police around all the time?"

"We're getting close to the end of the trial," Mom replied. "It's a crucial time and I guess I just feel better knowing you're safe."

"Why can't I go to Charlie's house for a play date?"

"It's just a precaution, hon."

"That's why I can't even walk home from school with my friends?"

She nodded. I didn't know whether to believe her or not. "Mom, honest, are we in some kind of danger?"

Mom looked straight back at me and didn't blink. "Don't you think I'd tell you if we were?"

At school my friends talked about seeing Mom on the news. But I wasn't allowed to go to their houses to play. They asked me to get her autograph. I'd bring them signatures I'd forged. How was I supposed to get autographs from her when I hardly even saw her myself?

At home Benjy and I beat every level of Dual Quantum U-Race and got bored with it. Benjy was doing the climbing wall in gym class at school. He came up with the idea of climbing our house from the first floor to the third floor without touching the ground. It wasn't as crazy as it sounded. We lived in a three-story town house with high ceilings. The first-floor stairs were modern and open underneath. You could hang from under the steps and pull yourself up. Like a rock climber pulling himself up under an overhang.

At the top of the first-floor stairs you could climb up onto the rail and inch your way along the second-floor landing until you reached the doorway that led to the third floor.

The next part was tricky. You had to climb off the rail and press your hands and feet against the insides of the doorway. The stairs to the third floor were narrow, with walls on both sides. You literally had to climb the walls—straight up the stairwell. Finally you reached the third floor by climbing over the banister.

"On your mark!" I yelled.

Benjy finished rosining his hands and dropped the rosin bag.

"Get set! Go!" I pressed the button on my stopwatch.

Benjy started to pull himself up the underside of the stairs. He was so light he went almost halfway up before he took a rest, hanging by one hand, then the other.

"Twenty-five seconds," I said.

With another burst of energy, Benjy climbed to the top rung of the first-floor stairs. Another rest period followed. Then he went into a tuck and slid one leg through the top rung. That allowed him to free one hand and then the other to grab on to the bottom of the rail along the second-floor landing. He was now hanging from the outside of the rail, twelve feet above the first floor.

Next came a pure-strength move—hand over hand up the side of the rail to the top. Then a pause for another rest.

"Two minutes!" I called as Dewey and I walked up the stairs the normal way.

Benjy crawled along the top of the second-floor rail like a caterpillar on a thin straight branch. When he reached the end I thought he'd rest, but he grabbed the edge of the open door and used it to steady himself as he rose to his feet on the rail. Then he stepped onto the doorknob and swung into the doorway.

"Two minutes, thirty-five seconds," I yelled. "A new world-record pace!"

The next move was tricky. Benjy had to grab the upper edge of the molding above the doorway, then swing his feet into the stairwell. I had twice been disqualified here for losing my grip and dropping to the third-floor stairs.

Benjy executed the move flawlessly.

"Two minutes, fifty seconds!" I cried.

My brother had entered the final stretch. Pressing a foot and a hand against either side of the stairwell, he inched his way straight up until he reached the lip of wood on the third floor. Then he rested again.

Ding dong! It was the front doorbell.

Groof! Pearson let out a bark and bounded out of the kitchen.

"Should we get it?" Dewey asked.

"As soon as Benjy breaks the world record," I said.

"How am I doing?" Benjy asked, hanging above us.

"Three minutes, forty-five seconds," I said.

Ding dong! The dumb doorbell rang again.

Groof! Pearson barked and scratched at the inside of the door.

"I thought no one was allowed to come here," said Benjy.

"Look, are you gonna break the world record or talk?" I knew he was tired and stalling.

"My hands are slipping," Benjy complained.

"Time!" I paused the stopwatch then ran downstairs and got the rosin bag. Rosin was allowed, just like in the Olympics.

Wedged above us in the stairwell, Benjy took the bag and rosined one hand at a time.

"Four minutes, twenty-five seconds." I restarted the clock.

Benjy grabbed the bottom of the third-floor rail and walked his feet up the wall. Then he inched his hands up and slid over the top of the railing, dropping in a heap to the third floor.

"Five minutes, seventeen seconds," I yelled. "A new world record!"

Ding dong!

Groof!

It was time to see who was at the door.

Better let me see first." Dewey went ahead and peeked through the spy hole.

Meanwhile, Benjy caught up to me. "Look, I'm sweating!"

I looked down at him. "Where?"

Benjy pointed to his forehead. A few strands of hair were clumped together and hung down in little blond points.

"I don't see any sweat," I said.

"It went into the hair," he said.

"Then it doesn't count."

"Aw, come on." Benjy pouted.

Dewey turned to me. "You better take a look." Through the spy hole I saw a balding man with a fringe of gray hair around the sides of his head. He was wearing a dark jacket and a tie, and carrying a big flat black briefcase. Standing beside him was one of the policemen who watched our house.

"Who is it?" I asked.

"Frederick Slater," the man replied. "The decorator."

"The what?" I said.

"From Burlington and Slater," he replied. "I have an appointment with Mrs. Marks. It's about the Bear River house."

Bear River house?

"Are you sure you have the right address?" I asked.

"Is this the Marks residence?" he asked back. "Megan and James Marks?"

"Yes."

"Mrs. Marks asked me to stop by around nine P.M.," Frederick Slater said. "It's nine oh five now."

I deactivated the alarm, undid the lock and sliding bolt, and opened the door.

"Thank you." Mr. Slater stood in the doorway looking a little peeved. The policeman went back to his car.

Pearson, his tail wagging, nudged his way through our legs and started to sniff Mr. Slater, who instantly stiffened. You could see he didn't like dogs.

"Back off, Pearson." I grabbed him by the collar and pulled him back.

Mr. Slater stepped into the house and looked

around. "Excuse me for being nosy, but do you always have policemen guarding your home?"

"It's because of the Nut Bombers," Benjy said.

"I'm sorry?" Mr. Slater scowled.

"The Nut Bombers who were going to blow up the government," Benjy explained. "Our mom is gonna put them away."

Mr. Slater's eyes widened for a moment. "Oh, I see."

Benjy turned back to Dewey. "You want to try?"

"You bet," Dewey said. They went back to the stairs. Dewey rosined his hands, then grabbed the rungs from underneath and started to pull himself up. Mr. Slater watched, sort of mystified.

"Anyway, my mom's not here," I said. "She usually doesn't get home this early."

Mr. Slater's forehead wrinkled. He was still watching Dewey go hand over hand up the stairs from underneath. "She said nine o'clock."

Mom was always making appointments she couldn't keep. People were always waiting for her.

"Uh, maybe you'd like to use the bathroom?" I asked.

Mr. Slater blinked. "No, thank you."

"Then maybe you'd like something to eat?" I was praying he'd say no since all we had was cereal, milk, orange juice, and ice cream.

"That's very kind, but no, thank you," said Mr.

Slater. He glanced out the corner of his eye toward the door. I had a feeling he wanted to go. Mom had taught me to try to keep them around until she got home.

"So what's this Bear River thing?" I asked.

"I'm sorry?" said Mr. Slater.

"You said something about a house," I reminded him.

"The one your parents just purchased," Mr. Slater said, putting down the flat briefcase. "I'm going to decorate it."

Benjy, who half-listened to everything, turned. "Like a cake?"

"A cake," Mr. Slater repeated, more to himself than to us. His eyes darted left and right as if he were checking to make sure he knew his way out of this nuthouse. "We decorate with furniture and window treatments and wallpaper. You've seen our showroom, haven't you? Next to McKinley's on Flag Street."

"McKinley's grocery store?" I said.

"That's right." Mr. Slater nodded.

Now I knew where he worked. Burlington & Slater was full of old furniture and mirrors. On the tables were big books filled with wallpaper samples. It was one of those totally boring stores Mom couldn't go past without looking inside.

"What's it like?" I asked.

"What's what like?" Mr. Slater replied.

"The house."

"Oh, fabulous. Log-style, but brand new. Nestled on the side of a hill overlooking the river. Utterly captivating."

Dewey made it halfway up the stairs, then hung for a while, looking tired.

"Why did they buy it?" Benjy asked.

Mr. Slater greeted each of our questions with a blink and a scowl, as if none of them made any sense to him. It was pretty obvious he didn't deal much with kids. "Why, to live in, I would imagine."

"We're moving?" Benjy and I gasped at the same time.

"Oh, no, I wouldn't think so," Mr. Slater said. "I'm sure it's just a weekend place. Mrs. Marks spoke of wanting something quiet and peaceful to get away to."

I think Benjy and I were a little shocked that our parents had bought a house and not even bothered to tell us. Then again maybe we shouldn't have been surprised. Anyway, we ran out of questions to ask, and an uncomfortable silence fell over the living room. We all watched Dewey climb the rest of the way up under the stairs, then grab the bottom of the second-floor rail.

Mr. Slater checked his watch. "Maybe I should go."

"You *sure* you don't need to use the bathroom?" I asked.

"Yes, I'm quite sure, thank you." He turned toward the door. Just then it opened and Mom rushed in.

"Oh, Mr. Slater." She breathlessly reactivated the alarm. "I'm so sorry I'm late."

"I could come back another time," Mr. Slater suggested.

"Oh, no. I came home early especially to take care of this," Mom said.

Mr. Slater's eyebrows rose slightly. "This is early?"

"If my kids are still up, it's early." Mom put down her bags. She stopped and stared at Dewey dangling in the air from the bottom of the second-floor railing.

"Hey, Mrs. Marks." Dewey briefly let go with one hand, waved, then grabbed the rail again.

Mom frowned.

Then she turned back to Mr. Slater. "Please, let's go into the living room."

I watched her lead Mr. Slater away. She'd come home early for *him?* How come she never came home early for *us?*

"What's the story, Mom?" I asked later. Mr. Slater had finally packed up his drawings and designs and left. Mom, Benjy, and I were heading upstairs to bed.

"I wanted it to be a surprise," Mom said. "It's the most beautiful place. Only an hour and a half from here, but you feel like you're a thousand miles away."

We reached the second-floor landing. Mom put her hand on the rail, then pulled it away and rubbed her fingers. "Why's the rail all sticky?"

Benjy shrugged and shot me a glance. It was the rosin. Mom stared at her fingers. You could almost see her thoughts going back to Dewey hanging from the railing earlier. She pursed her lips angrily.

"No more climbing," she said sternly. "I do *not* want this house turned into a jungle gym. Do I make myself clear?"

"Sure, Mom," Benjy said. "So when can we go to our new house?"

"Soon." Mom calmed down pretty fast.

"When is soon?" I asked.

"As soon as your Dad and I find the time."

Benjy and I shared a doubtful look. As far as we were concerned, that meant never.

8

Dad looks exactly like the overworked weary business traveler you always see in those commercials for hotel chains, airlines, and rental cars. Only he's not the smooth-looking hero who uses the right company and gets to travel in comfort. He's the other guy—the overweight, bald, wrinkled one who picks the wrong company and winds up sitting next to the weirdo in the monkey suit or sleeping in the motel room next to the rumbling ice machine or wandering around the parking lot in the middle of a rainstorm looking for his rental car.

Not that he's a loser or anything. He's an expert in laying telephone cable, and the kind of person other people always seem pleased to say hello to when they see him at the store or movies. He isn't much of an athlete and doesn't watch sports on TV. In fact, he hardly ever watches TV at all. Like Mom, he's totally involved in his work.

Dad came home from Asia and slept for a whole day. Over the weekend he took us to a baseball game (because Benjy begged him) and to a movie. On Sunday night we all went out to his favorite Chinese restaurant.

"Aren't you a little tired of this stuff?" I asked him as the waiters brought us plates of sesame chicken, moo-shoo pork, beef with broccoli, and sautéed string beans.

"Why would I be tired of it?" Dad asked as he dunked a piece of egg roll into a small dish of sweet and sour sauce.

"Because you just ate it for three weeks," I said.

Dad smiled. "Steven, I didn't see an egg roll, a crispy noodle, or a spare rib the whole time I was there."

"But this is Chinese food," said Benjy.

"No." Dad shook his head. "This is what we Americans call Chinese food. The food over there is completely different."

"So what do you eat over there?" I asked.

"A lot of vegetables and noodles," Dad said. "And if you want to go out for something special you might have hairy crab or chicken with the claws still on."

"Gross!" Benjy wrinkled his nose in disgust.

From somewhere in her clothes came the chime of Mom's cell phone. "Oh, darn." She took it out of her pocket. "Hello?" she answered, barely above a whisper. "Oh, hi, Jack. Give me a second." She got up and headed for the ladies' room. Mom was embarrassed about getting cell-phone calls in public places.

"What's fascinating is that Bangkok is a fully developed modern city," Dad went on. "But as soon as you leave, it's like stepping back in time one hundred years."

"What do you mean?" Benjy asked.

"In the country they don't have cars," Dad explained. "They don't go to movies or out to eat. Most of them don't even have telephones in their homes."

"What about TVs?"

"Everyone has a TV," Dad said.

"Do they have families?" Benjy asked.

Dad scowled. "I don't follow."

"Do they have moms and dads at home?" Benjy said.

"Of course." Dad's face changed as he understood Benjy's question. "So, it bothers you that I'm away so much."

Benjy and I nodded.

"It won't be forever," he said. "It's just that they have a different way of doing things over there and we

44

have to be on-site to make sure they're meeting our specs."

"Can't you get someone else to do it?" Benjy asked.

"Bill Griffin's there right now," Dad said. "But he has a family too. I'll be around this week, but then I have to go back."

"Will you be around the house this week, or at the office?" I asked.

"Well, at the office mostly," Dad admitted. "I've got a lot of catching up to do."

"Can't someone else go to Thailand next?" Benjy asked.

"No," Dad said. "It's my project; my responsibility."

It sounded just like when Mom talked about her responsibilities. But whose responsibility were we?

Mom came out of the ladies' room and sat down. "Sorry about that. Jack needed some hand-holding."

"Why?" I asked.

"He gets worried," Mom said. "Then he wants me to reassure him that our case is airtight. Of course, it *isn't*. But I have to reassure him anyway."

"Makes you wonder why *he's* the boss and not you," Dad quipped.

"Well, maybe someday . . ." Mom replied with a wink.

"Wait a minute," I said. "I thought you promised that after this trial you were going to take a long time off and be with us."

Mom looked surprised, then quickly recovered. "That's exactly what I plan to do."

"You can't do that *and* get Jack's job," I pointed out.

"Hush!" Mom's eyes darted left and right as if some spy in the restaurant might have heard me. "I was kidding. I'm not going after Jack's job. That's the *last* thing I want."

Was I really supposed to believe her?

Dad picked up the half-finished platter of moo-shoo pork. "Anyone still hungry?"

The rest of us shook our heads. Dad dumped the remaining moo-shoo pork on his plate, doused it with sauce, and dug in.

"Hon?" Mom said.

"Hmmm?" Dad sort of grunted with his mouth full.

"That's your third helping."

"It's Chinese," Dad replied. "I'll be hungry again in an hour."

"You've been gaining weight."

"Me?" Dad looked surprised, then turned to Benjy and me. "Tell the truth, have I gained any weight?"

Benjy and I both nodded. I'd noticed earlier that his

middle had started to hang over his belt . . . on all sides.

"See?" Mom said.

Dad chewed slowly, then swallowed. "All right, after work tomorrow I'm going to the gym."

Dad rarely left his office before seven o'clock. If he went to the gym, that would add another hour and a half to his day. Which meant he'd be home just in time to say good night to us.

Dad went to the office for a week, then left for Thailand again. The Nut Bomber trial dragged on. If anything, we saw even less of Mom than before. Unless you counted TV. Almost every night on the news we saw her and the other prosecutors at their table in the courtroom. The table was covered with books and papers and laptop computers. Mom and the other prosecutors wrote notes on long yellow pads of paper and whispered to one another.

Meanwhile, Dewey stayed with us each evening until Mom got home, and again each morning between the time she went to work and when we went to school. Sometimes I pretended we were on a desert island. Just me, Benjy, and Dewey.

"Is there any milk?" Benjy yelled into the kitchen

one evening. We were in the den, watching TV and eating SpaghettiOs. Dewey was in the kitchen.

"Coming, Benjo tart." Dewey came into the den with two glasses of milk.

"I meant chocolate milk," Benjy said with a yawn. We'd been up past eleven P.M. the night before, watching *Animal House.* Now we were watching a news show about a father who kidnapped his own kids.

Dewey went back into the kitchen to find the chocolate syrup.

"How come the father had to kidnap his own kids?" Benjy asked me.

"He and the mom were divorced and he didn't like the way she was raising them," I explained. "So he took them away."

"Could he get in trouble?"

"I don't know," I said. "I mean, they're *his* kids too."

"Maybe we should kidnap our parents," Benjy mused.

I looked at Dewey in the kitchen, going through the cabinets. Then I looked back at my brother. In my head I saw our parents tied to chairs, blindfolded, and gagged.

"Could *we* get in trouble?" Benjy asked with another yawn.

"I don't know," I said.

Dewey came back. "That's a negative on the chocolate syrup, Benjo."

"Then I'm not eating." Benjy crossed his arms.

"You can still consume your spaghetti," Dewey said.

Benjy shook his head stubbornly. Dewey sat down and stared at the TV. Normally the nanny would have gone up to McKinley's and gotten syrup. With Dewey it wasn't worth trying to explain. Besides, I was tired of being locked in the house all the time. I wanted to get out. I got up and took some money off the kitchen counter. Dewey and Benjy were staring at the TV. Neither of them noticed when I left.

To get out without the police seeing me, I had to go into the bathroom behind the kitchen, climb up onto the toilet, and slide open the narrow window behind it. I managed to squeeze through, grab on to a drainpipe, and slide down to the ground. Next I hopped a couple of fences and snuck around a town house three houses away. Suddenly, for the first time in weeks, I was walking along the sidewalk by myself. It felt great to be free.

A few minutes later I left McKinley's with the chocolate syrup in a brown paper bag. I wished I had someplace else to go, but I didn't. Besides, I didn't want to risk getting into trouble.

Heading back down the sidewalk, I was passing Burlington & Slater when I noticed a dented red pickup truck parked outside. Two scruffy-looking men were sitting inside the truck. One had short blond hair and a long bushy beard. The other had wild, uncombed black hair. Dark stubble covered his chin. Both were wearing old, tattered olive-colored Army surplus jackets.

I'm not sure why I noticed them. Maybe it was because we lived in a pretty nice neighborhood and you rarely saw old beat-up trucks around. Or maybe it was the way the two men stared so intently into the decorators' shop. They definitely didn't look like the type of people who would be interested in window treatments.

My interest in them faded as soon as I passed their truck. I was in a hurry now. A slight sense of nervousness had replaced the giddiness I'd felt at first escaping from my house. Now I was worried that Dewey might notice I was missing and sound the alarm.

I retraced my steps back through the yards and over the fences. Clenching the brown paper bag in my teeth, I shimmied up the drainpipe and squeezed back through the bathroom window. All in all, I doubted I'd been gone for more than ten minutes.

Back in the den, Dewey was still watching the TV.

"I got the chocolate syrup." I slid the bottle of syrup out of the brown bag.

"Too late," Dewey said without taking his eyes off the TV.

"What do you mean?" I asked.

He pointed into the living room. Benjy was lying on his stomach on the couch, fast asleep. His eyes were closed and his mouth was open. One of his arms hung limply over the edge.

It was only 6:20 in the evening.

"Guess he was tired," Dewey said with a shrug.

"I guess." I flipped the bottle of chocolate in the air. "So aren't you going to ask how I got it?"

"Got what?" He still hadn't moved his eyes from the TV.

"The chocolate syrup."

Dewey shook his head.

"Come on, Dewey, how do you think I got it?" I asked.

Dewey finally turned and looked at me. "You found it?"

"I bought it," I said proudly. "I snuck out."

Dewey blinked. "You snuck out of the *house?*"

"Yup."

Dewey smirked. "Very funny, Stevenski. You want to get me busted, bone brain? That's the one thing your mother said I was never, *ever* allowed to let you or Benjamin do."

"Who's going to tell her?" I sat down in the chair next to him.

Dewey glanced at Benjy asleep on the couch, then looked back at me and smiled. "Okay, Houdini, but you gotta promise never to do that again, ever. Otherwise I'll get the boot and you'll get another Nazi nanny."

He was probably right. Dewey looked back at the TV. The weather lady was on.

"How old are you, Dewey?" I asked.

"Uh, twenty-two," Dewey answered, again not taking his eyes off the TV.

"How come you don't go to college or have a job or anything?" I asked.

"That's not my thing," Dewey replied. "Nine to five is a boring drive."

"You have to do *something,* don't you?" I said.

"I got some ideas," Dewey said. "Being an investigative reporter would be cool. Or driving an ambulance. Or maybe joining the police auxiliary."

"What's that?"

"You help the police with patrols and community

crime watch and junk. And you get in on the cool stuff, too. Like disasters and fires."

"But it's not like they let you have a gun, right?" I asked. The idea of Dewey with a gun was *totally* scary.

"Naw." Dewey shook his head. "I have a few cop things I bought on my own, like a nightstick and some handcuffs. But no guns."

We watched the rest of the weather. Then some commercials came on.

"Remember that thing before about the father who kidnapped his own kids?" I asked.

"Yeah."

"Could he get into trouble?"

"Sure, sonny. They had a custody agreement and he broke it."

"Suppose some kids wanted to kidnap their own parents?" I said. "Could they get into trouble?"

Dewey made a face. "What would they want to do that for?"

"Just pretend," I said.

"Well . . . I bet their parents would be pretty ticked."

"I meant, could the kids get in trouble with the police?"

Dewey pressed his chin into his hand. "Well, I don't know, Stevenski. I mean, it's not like the parents would press charges against their own kids. But they'd definitely get heavily grounded."

Yeah? So? I found myself thinking. I wasn't supposed to leave the house. I wasn't allowed to go on play dates. So I was already grounded.

And I'd never done anything to deserve it.

I couldn't get the idea of kidnapping Mom and Dad out of my head. I know it probably sounds weird. Half the kids I knew wished they *didn't* have to spend time with their parents. But then, their parents usually came home before midnight.

Then one night Mom surprised us by coming home early with a pizza.

"I have good news and bad news," she said as she put slices on plates. The pizza was half pepperoni (Benjy's favorite) and half sausage and mushroom (my favorite). "The good news is that closing arguments will begin next week. That means the trial really will be ending soon."

Benjy and I rolled our eyes in a united display of disbelief. *"Sure,* Mom."

"You'll see." Mom smiled. "And there's more

good news. I need to get away and have peace and quiet while I prepare my closing summary. Your father's plane from Seoul lands Friday afternoon around four, and we've decided to go straight from the airport to our new country house for the weekend."

Benjy's forehead wrinkled. "What about us?"

"All of us, silly," Mom said. "We'll all go for the weekend."

"So what's the bad news?" I asked.

"The final arguments are the most intense part of the trial," she said. "I may not even be able to get home some nights."

"Figures," I mumbled.

"Don't say that, Steven," Mom said. "I'm being completely honest. And as I said before, as soon as the trial is over, things are going to be very different."

"Why?" Benjy asked.

"I can't really talk about it now," Mom said. "You'll just have to trust me."

This time I kept my thoughts to myself. As if I'd never heard *that one* before. The truth was, I didn't trust her. As far as I could see, nothing was going to change. Not unless Benjy and I did something to make it change.

• • •

"Ready?" Dewey called from the second-floor landing.

"Ready," I called back from down in the living room.

It was the night before we were supposed to go to our new country house. I'd talked Dewey into bringing over some of his police auxiliary stuff, including some safety ropes and two sets of real handcuffs.

We'd strung one of the ropes from the railing on the second-floor landing down to a column at the far end of the living room. Dewey showed us how to make a harness out of the other rope.

"Ready, Benjo?" Dewey asked.

"Ready," said Benjy, who was wearing the rope harness and sitting on the second-floor railing.

"Let her rip!" Dewey shouted.

Benjy let go of railing. Holding on to the harness, he sailed out over the front hall, into the living room, over the couch and coffee table, and down to the column, where I caught him.

"Way cool!" he cried.

"My turn!" I quickly climbed up the stairs. Dewey showed me how to get into the harness. A moment later I was sailing down through the house.

We did that for a while and then wanted to fool

around with some of the other stuff. I was particularly interested in the handcuffs. They were made of steel, with thick chain linking them together. Each set came with its own key.

While the three of us sat at the kitchen table, fooling around with the cuffs, I told Dewey my plan.

"No, forget it. No way." Dewey shook his head when I'd finished.

"You won't get in trouble," I said. "I *promise*. I won't tell anyone where I got them. I *swear.*"

"*Please?*" Benjy begged.

"No," Dewey kept saying. "I can't. These things cost serious dollars. You guys are totally wacked."

"It's not fair," I complained. "*You* got to have a mom and a dad when you were our age."

"But—"

"I bet *your* mom made *you* breakfast," Benjy said accusingly.

"Sure, but—"

"We just want to borrow the handcuffs," I said. "We won't even tell Mom and Dad where we got them. And I *swear,* if I lose them, I'll pay you back."

Dewey looked out the kitchen window into the dark.

"I promise, Dewey," I pleaded. "They'll never know

where we got them. I *swear.* And no matter what happens, I'll pay you back."

I don't think Benjy or I quite believed it the next day when Mom picked us up at school.

"Where's Mr. Sam?" Benjy asked, looking around outside.

"You don't need him, silly," Mom said. "I'm here."

"You mean, we're *really* going away for the weekend?" I asked.

"Of course we are," Mom said. "I *told* you we were."

Benjy and I shared a look. I think we'd both expected to find Mr. Sam waiting for us after school with a message from Mom that "something unexpected" had come up. I mean, "something unexpected" *always* came up.

But not this time.

We got into the car and drove to the airport to pick up Dad. Pearson's leash was lying on the floor. It had a heavy-duty plastic handle with a grip. The leash itself was about fifteen feet long and made of plastic-covered wire. When Pearson wasn't hooked to it, the wire wound up inside the handle.

"Where's Pearson?" Benjy asked.

"I just dropped him at the kennel," Mom said.

"Couldn't he come too?" I asked.

"There's no room in the car."

"That's not fair," Benjy complained. "He's part of the family."

"Where would he sit?" Mom asked.

"Back here with Steven and me," said Benjy.

Even I knew that wouldn't work. Pearson would have climbed all over us.

We got to the airport and waited in the car outside the terminal doors. Mom chattered excitedly about the new house and the meadow and woods and how neat it would be to take walks and fish in the Bear River and stuff. I have to admit she really got Benjy and me psyched about the weekend. We were finally getting away from the city, away from the police outside our house all the time, away from all the rest of the Nut Bomber craziness. For once Mom was keeping her word.

Dad came out of the airline terminal carrying a long fat tube filled with blueprints and pulling his black suitcase on wheels behind him. He put the suitcase and tube in the trunk, then got into the front seat.

He gave Mom a quick kiss. "Jack's okay with this?"

"He's not thrilled." Mom started to drive. "But I convinced him we'd be okay. After all, no one knows about this place."

Dad looked over the seat at Benjy and me.

"Excited?" he asked.

Benjy and I nodded. *Amazed* was probably a better word to describe how we really felt.

"We're going to have a great time," Dad said.

We left the airport and went north on the highway for a while, then followed some narrower roads that led up into the hills. Benjy and I watched through the windows as we passed ranches, fenced meadows, and big patches of scrub and pine. Finally we came to a small convenience store with a porch and a pay phone outside. We turned up a gravel road toward an old steel bridge.

"The Bear River," Dad said, nodding down at the fast-moving rapids below the bridge. Downstream the river broadened and grew smoother before disappearing around a bend.

On the other side of the bridge, the grade of the gravel road grew steeper, going uphill next to a broad meadow filled with tall wheat-colored grass. Mom made a right turn up a dirt driveway and stopped before the biggest log cabin I'd ever seen.

"Oh, wow!" Benjy pressed his face against the car window. "Is this it?"

"Sure is," Dad said with a grin.

We got out to take a closer look. It wasn't a cabin but a big two-story log house with large picture windows, and a wide deck in front. The logs were shiny and the color of vanilla pudding. The sun was starting to go down and it bathed the front of the house in reddish light, turning the big windows dark green.

"Is it really ours?" Benjy asked.

Mom nodded. "This is where we'll come to get away from everything and just be a family together."

"And lose a little weight." Dad patted his middle.

We went inside. The house smelled like pine spray. The first floor was mostly a big open room with a tall stone fireplace in the middle going right up through the ceiling. A kitchen with shiny silver appliances was off to one side, and a long wooden table stood next to a wall of windows facing the meadow. All the tables and chairs in the room were made out of bent wood.

"What's upstairs?" I pointed to the other side of the house, where a staircase went up to a second-floor landing just like in our town house in the city.

"The bedrooms," Mom said. "And downstairs is the exercise and rec room."

"What about TV?" Benjy asked.

"In the rec room," Mom said.

Benjy and I took off down the stairs. The rec room was awesome. They'd put in a miniature pool table, a Ping-Pong table, a treadmill, and a totally cool TV. It was one of those wide-screen jobs hooked up to a satellite dish, and it pulled in so many channels that we couldn't stay on any single one for long without feeling tempted to surf through the others.

Benjy and I watched TV until we got hungry, and I went upstairs to see what there was to eat. Mom was sitting in a chair next to the fireplace with a bunch of papers spread out on the coffee table beside her. Dad was sitting at the long, wide kitchen table with a bunch of blueprints spread out before him.

I stopped and stared in disbelief.

They were working.

They hadn't even gotten out of their work clothes.

It was just like home.

"I thought you weren't going to work here," I said.

Mom and Dad locked eyes across the room.

"I warned them that I was going to have to spend most of the weekend preparing my summary statement," Mom said. "Maybe you could do something with them."

Dad shook his head. "I can't. You know those cable

monitoring stations we're putting up every ten miles through the jungle? Just before I left Penang, the foreman on the construction crew took me into one of the bathrooms and showed me that the countertop was too high for his men. Bill designed them to American specs, but your average Asian worker isn't as tall as his American counterpart."

"Which means?" Mom said.

"Ripping out all the counters and cutting them down," Dad said. "And replumbing the faucets and sink drains. But that's the least of it. What about water fountains? And the height we set for doorknobs? What about the windows, and the shelving in the tool closets? Handrails and worktables . . . It goes on and on. I have to rethink this whole thing over the weekend and head back over there on Tuesday."

"You're going back to Thailand in *three* days?" I was stunned.

"I have no choice," Dad replied.

It was the same old thing. . . . Dad may have been doing great things for communication around the world, but he sure wasn't much on communicating with his own kids. It was hopeless.

I looked back at Mom. "What's there to eat?"

"Check the fridge," she said. "There are all kinds of cold cuts. And I want you and Benjy to have milk."

I opened the refrigerator. Inside were some packages of cold cuts and cheese, a couple of quarts of milk, and some pears and oranges. I opened some of the cupboards, but they were empty.

"Where's the rest of the food?" I asked.

"In the trunk of the car, probably." Mom reached into her bag and held up some keys. I took them and went out to the car. In the trunk were two cardboard boxes filled with bread, cereal, pancake mix, spaghetti, and other stuff.

I brought the boxes into the kitchen and put them on the counter. At the bottom of one of the boxes I found a package of Oreos and a bag of chocolate-chip cookies. Suddenly I didn't feel like having cold cuts. I took the chocolate-chip cookies, along with a quart of milk and some glasses, and went back down to the rec room. Mom didn't even look up.

Benjy and I had our own rooms with double-decker bunk beds for when we invited friends to visit. But that night we both stayed in my room.

We slept late the next morning. When we got up and went downstairs, Mom was sitting by the fireplace again with her papers spread out on the coffee table. She was wearing jeans and a heavy red sweatshirt with a hood, but on her feet were those shiny black shoes with the narrow heels.

"What's with the shoes?" I asked.

Mom smiled ruefully. "I forgot to pack a comfortable pair. So I'm stuck with these for the weekend. Anyway, I've been waiting for you. Give me a second and I'll make you a nice big country breakfast."

You could see this was something she'd been planning. A few minutes later, she closed the folder on her lap and went over to the kitchen counter and cooked up a big breakfast of Oreo pancakes, fresh-squeezed orange juice, and bacon. We sat down on the opposite end of the kitchen table from where Dad's blueprints were still spread.

"Isn't this incredible?" Mom asked. Through the windows we could see the tall wheat-colored grass of the meadow, the trees, the Bear River valley, the hills on the other side of it, and the distant snowcapped mountains beyond them.

"Yeah, it's really amazing," I said. "But where's Dad?"

"I think he's on the treadmill downstairs," Mom said. "He really wants to get back into shape."

"So what are we gonna do today?" Benjy asked as he mopped up some maple syrup with his last piece of pancake.

"Well, we thought we'd take a ride into the mountains later," Mom answered.

"What about now?" I asked.

"Well, uh, remember I told you about my closing summary?" Mom asked.

"You worked on it last night," I said.

"I still have more to do," Mom said. "Why don't you two go outside and explore?"

"Mom, this is ridiculous," I sputtered. "You said we were going to come up here to get away from all the work. Instead, you and Dad just brought it all with you. I don't even know why Dad bothered to come home. All he's gonna do is work and go back to Thailand again in three days."

Tweeeeet! Mom's cell phone chirped. She reached down to the coffee table and picked it up. "Oh, hi, Jack . . . Yes, we need to plan this out . . . Can you hold on a moment?" Mom put her hand over the phone. "Why don't you get dressed and go outside with Benjy, hon? This is going to take a while."

"But—"

"It's Jack, hon, I really have to talk to him."

"Right." I nodded and turned away. We may have been in a different place for the weekend, but nothing had changed.

Benjy and I went upstairs and got dressed. When we went back downstairs, Mom was in the chair beside the fireplace, still talking on her cell phone. She waved as we went outside.

The sun was bright and the air smelled fresh. Everything seemed clearer than in the city. We walked down to the end of the driveway and looked around. A large hill covered with dense pine rose up behind our new house. There wasn't another house or person in sight, just the convenience store way down the road on the other side of the bridge.

"Isn't this great?" Benjy asked.

"For who?" I asked back.

Benjy studied me. "You're mad 'cause Mom's working?"

I nodded. "Nothing's changed. I guarantee you

this afternoon she'll have some excuse why we can't drive into the mountains. They're both going to work all day."

"Maybe they have to," Benjy said.

"They *always* have to," I shot back. "Even when they're with us they're really just working with us around." I looked back at the house. The handcuffs were in my bag in my room. "I say we do it, Benjy."

Benjy bit his lip nervously. "I don't know, Steven. They're gonna be so mad."

"Yeah, so? At least it'll get them to pay attention to us for once."

Benjy looked down at the ground and nudged a rock with his toe. "But we don't need them here. We could have fun without them."

"And then go back home and have no one to take care of us except Dewey and Mr. Sam," I reminded him.

My brother looked up at me. "How would we do it anyway?"

I told him my plan. I could tell he wasn't happy about it, but I needed his help. It took a while, but I finally convinced him that if we didn't do something, nothing was ever going to change. We'd wake up every morning for the rest of our lives with only yesterday's wrinkled clothes to wear, junky breakfasts to eat, and unsigned permission slips so we couldn't go on cool field trips.

"When do you want to do it?" he asked.

"Right now." Even as I said it, a bolt of nervousness raced through me.

"Can't we wait until later?" Benjy asked.

"No. We'll chicken out," I said. "We have to do it now. If we don't, nothing's ever going to change."

Benjy stared at me uncertainly.

"Come on," I said. We started to walk back up the driveway. I stopped at the car and got out Pearson's extra retractable leash.

Back in the house, I got the handcuffs out of my book bag. I put one pair in my pocket and gave Benjy the other pair.

"Let's go," I whispered, and led him down the stairs. We stopped beside the big stone hearth in the middle of the main room. The fireplace was open on two ends. Through it we could see Mom sitting in her chair on the other side. Sticking out of the stone on our side were some iron loops for hanging the fire tools. I hooked the clip of the leash to one of them.

"Go around to the other side of the fireplace," I whispered to Benjy. "Pretend you're being an Army man."

Benjy did what he was told. Letting the wire leash unroll from the retractor, I passed the heavy-duty plastic handle through the fireplace and under the iron rack cemented in the middle. Benjy reached in from the other side and took it. Then I motioned him to come back.

"Okay, here's what you're going to do," I whispered. "Tell Mom you want to be handcuffed to her so you can be close. Make it seem like a game. Tell her they're just toy handcuffs. Keep whining until she lets you do it. Close one cuff around her wrist and the other around the handle of the leash."

Benjy chewed anxiously on his thumbnail. "I'm scared."

"Look, I already told you they're gonna get mad and yell," I whispered. "They're going to threaten us and say they're going to punish us and everything. But they'll never really do it."

"Why not?" Benjy asked.

"Because deep inside they'll know we're right," I whispered. "They'll be mad for a while. But then they'll forgive us."

I'm not sure Benjy believed me, but he nodded anyway.

"Now remember," I whispered, pointing to my wristwatch, "it won't work unless we both do it at the exact same time. It's 10:31. Start working on Mom at 10:35. By 10:40 you have to have her handcuffed."

Benjy winced at the thought. "They're gonna be so mad."

"Do they ever spend time with you?" I asked.

"Not much." Benjy shrugged.

"I guarantee you they will after this."

I left Benjy and went downstairs to the rec room. Dad was on the treadmill, huffing and puffing as he jogged. Holding the handrails for balance, he was reading some papers propped up on the plastic reading rack over the treadmill's digital display.

His forehead was dotted with perspiration. A big wet bib-shaped sweat stain covered the front of his gray T-shirt.

"Hey, Dad," I said, fingering the handcuffs in my pocket.

"Hey, Steven," he answered.

"Whatcha reading?"

"Work stuff. What're you and Benjy doing?"

"Playing Army," I said.

Dad nodded and looked back down at his papers. I slowly took the handcuffs out of my pocket and clipped one cuff around the rail behind his left hand. I waited for a second to see if he noticed, but he didn't.

My hands were trembling as I held the other cuff open.

Click! In one fast move I clipped it around Dad's wrist.

Still jogging, Dad looked down and frowned. "What's this?"

"Don't get mad, Dad," I said, then dashed out of the rec room.

Coming up the stairs from the rec room, I practically crashed into Benjy. He crept down to peek at Dad. His eyes were wide, and he looked scared and excited. Upstairs we ran past Mom. She was sitting next to the fireplace with her right arm extended. Her wrist was handcuffed to the handle of the wire dog leash, and the leash snaked through the fireplace to the iron ring on the other side.

"Undo this right now, boys," she said in that calm, controlled voice.

"You did it!" I said to my little brother.

He nodded.

"Great, let's go."

"Wait!" Mom called.

Benjy stopped. I grabbed his hand and pulled.

"Steven, Benjamin, where are you going?" Mom demanded. "You can't leave me like this."

I shoved Benjy through the front door and turned

back to her. "We'll be back, Mom. We just want you to get used to it."

"Used to what?" Mom asked.

"Being our prisoner." I went out the front door and pulled it closed behind me.

13

I led Benjy down to the end of the driveway. We turned left and started down the gravel road to the bridge over the Bear River. It was right around noon, and the sun was high overhead.

"You sweating?" Benjy asked.

I felt my forehead and under my armpits. Even though the sun seemed incredibly bright, it wasn't very warm out. "Not really."

"Me neither." He sounded disappointed.

"Don't worry, your day will come," I assured him.

He stopped and looked back up the road at the house. "We're just going to leave them like that?"

"For a while," I said. "Till they calm down."

Benjy tugged anxiously at his ear. "I'm scared, Steven. Mom and Dad are gonna be really mad."

"In a little while we'll go back and explain why we

did it," I said. "They'll *have* to understand. They're our parents."

"I never heard of anyone taking both their parents prisoner," Benjy said.

"That's because most kids don't *have* to," I explained. "Their parents are around. They *do* stuff with their kids."

"But why did we have to lock them up?" Benjy asked. "Why couldn't we just tell them?"

"Because we've already told them a million times," I said. "It never does any good. They promise to do stuff with us, but they never do. Or they do something really quick and get it over with so they can go back to work."

Benjy glanced back at the house again. "What do you think they're doing?"

"Probably trying to get free," I guessed. "Mom's probably trying to stretch toward the kitchen counter to see if she can find something to cut the leash with, but she won't come close. Dad's probably gotten off the treadmill. Maybe he's even dragged it to the door, but it's too big and heavy to get through the doorway and up the stairs."

"Then what?" Benjy asked.

"They'll start talking to each other," I said. "Like trying to figure out what's going on."

"And *then* what?" Benjy asked.

"Maybe they'll starting thinking about why we did it," I said.

We walked down to the bridge over the Bear River. North and south of the bridge, the river was wide and smooth. But under the bridge it narrowed and roared, splashing and foaming through the rocks.

We reached the bridge and stopped. I'd never seen a bridge like it. It was flat and straight on top, with a rail along either side to keep people from falling off. The underneath was crescent-shaped, starting from each shore and rising to its highest point under the middle.

I saw Benjy's lips move and knew he was saying something, but we were so close to the rapids that the roar of the water drowned out his words.

"What'd you say?" I shouted.

Benjy pointed to the bridge. "Wanna look under it?"

"Okay," I said.

My brother started down the steep riverbank of loose rocks and reddish dirt that disappeared into the racing water. Benjy's feet slid through the rocks and dirt. While it wasn't incredibly dangerous, I knew that if either of us lost our footing, we could tumble down into the rapids and be swept away.

As I followed him—my feet sinking into the dirt and

sliding with almost every step—I really had to wonder about Benjy. He was a funny kid. Scampering along the edge of these rapids, with that furious river roaring along less than a dozen feet away, didn't scare him at all.

But the sound of Mom's voice, especially when she was mad, terrified him.

The bridge was anchored at both ends by huge concrete blocks, each the size of a small truck. Ahead of me, Benjy stepped carefully around one of them and disappeared into the shadows under the bridge. I followed.

Under the bridge, the roar of the rapids echoed so loudly it sounded like a jet engine. The light was dim and the air was full of mist kicked up by the churning white water. Benjy sat on the rocky shore and tucked his knees up under his chin. A few yards away the water hurtled past.

I sat down next to him. Together we stared through the mist and shadows at the rapids. We didn't say anything. I'm not sure we could have heard each other anyway. We just sat there in the dim light under the bridge, enveloped by the roar and the mist.

Maybe it should have been scary, but it was a lot less scary than being back in the house with our parents.

• • •

After a while Benjy looked at me, and I could tell he was wondering if we should go back. We climbed out from under the bridge and scrambled over the loose rocks and dirt up the riverbank, then started up the gravel road toward the house.

Benjy didn't say a word.

But when we got to the place where our driveway met the road, he stopped and hugged himself.

"I'm scared," he said, gazing up at the house.

"Yeah, well, I'm a little freaked too," I admitted.

"They're going to be super mad," he said.

"Just remember: Sticks and stones can break your bones, but words can never hurt you." I started up the driveway. Benjy didn't budge. I looked back at him.

"You go," he said. "I'll wait here."

I looked up at the house. My heart started to pound, and my throat felt so tight it was hard to swallow. I could feel the blood pulsing under my scalp. I wasn't looking forward to facing my parents. But it was too late now to back out.

14

I walked slowly up the driveway. Even though the air was cool, the sun felt hot on the back of my head. As I neared the house, my heart seemed to beat even harder and my stomach felt like it wanted to rise up into my throat.

I reached the front door. It seemed bigger than it had before. My heart was banging so hard now I was starting to feel dizzy. I reached for the doorknob and was surprised at how hot it felt in the sun.

I turned the doorknob and pushed the door open.

Mom was sitting in the chair beside the fireplace, holding the phone, almost exactly the way she'd been before. Only now there were no papers on her lap.

"Welcome home," she said.

I nodded and closed the door behind me.

"Do you think you could let me go now?" she asked.

"*Meg?*" Dad called from downstairs.

"Steven's back," Mom replied. Then she turned to me. "Where's Benjy?"

"Outside," I said.

Mom raised her right hand, the one handcuffed to the handle of the leash. She raised her eyebrows as if to say, "Unlock me."

I shook my head.

"*What's going on?*" Dad called from the rec room.

"I'm not sure," Mom called back.

"*What?*"

"Give us a moment," she said, then turned to me again. "What's this about, Steven?"

"Benjy and I want to make a deal," I said. "We want you to be with us all weekend. No work."

"Listen to me, Steven," Mom said. "I just got a call from Jack. Something's come up and there's a meeting back in the city this afternoon. I know we promised you we'd spend the weekend, but I have to go back."

I shook my head.

"I don't think you understand." Mom went into her super-calm firm mode. "The defense wants to introduce new evidence. I *have* to attend that meeting."

"You always *have* to attend some meeting," I said. "You always *have* to work."

"Not always," Mom said.

"*Meg?*" Dad called from the rec room.

"Steven and I are talking," she called back.

"*Why can't he unlock me?*" Dad called.

Mom looked at me and raised her eyebrows again. I shook my head.

"He doesn't seem to want to!" Mom called down.

"*Steven!?*" Dad yelled.

The anger in his voice sent a shiver through me. It had been a long time since I'd heard him yell like that. Maybe not since I was Benjy's age. It made me feel small and frightened. The scared half of me wanted to go downstairs and unlock him right away. But the other half knew that if I did that now, nothing would ever change.

"*Steven, answer me!*" Dad shouted.

I locked eyes with Mom and took a step back toward the door.

"Don't, Steven," Mom said as calmly as she could.

"*Steven?*" Dad shouted from below.

I went out the door and pulled it closed behind me.

It was a relief to be outside and in the sunlight where Dad's angry voice couldn't reach me. On trembling legs, I walked back down the driveway. Benjy was sitting on a rock in the shade of a tree, playing with some pinecones. He looked up. "What happened?"

"Everything's okay," I said.

An astonished look passed over his face. "They're gonna stay with us and not work all weekend?"

"We're getting there," I said.

A scowl replaced the astonished look. "What's *that* mean?"

I sat down on the rock next to him. "Look, Benj, it's gonna take some time for them to get used to this. Big changes don't happen overnight."

Benjy stared down at the pinecones. "You mean they're really mad."

"They're not real happy," I admitted. "But it's not like they can do much about it."

"They can punish us," he said.

"How?"

"I don't know. Not take us places. Not let us out of the house."

"How's that different from the way things are now?" I asked.

Benjy didn't answer. He glanced up at the house. "What happens next?"

"We wait," I said.

"What's that gonna do?"

"Give them time to calm down and talk it over," I said.

"Maybe," said my brother. "But if one of them gets loose, they're gonna kill us."

It wasn't easy to wait. Ten minutes felt like forever. After fifteen minutes I couldn't stand it anymore. I walked up the driveway again, my heart pounding just like the last time. The scared half of me wanted to give up. But something wouldn't let me—that thing in me that needed to have them understand.

I opened the front door a little and peeked in. Mom was sitting in the chair by the fireplace. When she saw me, she nodded. "All right. We'll stay all weekend. No work."

"No telephones," I said.

"But we have to tell people where we are," she said. "I've got to call Jack back."

"I'll call him," I said.

Mom looked shocked. "You don't trust me?"

I started to shake my head, then stopped. "I trust you, Mom. Like I know you'd never do anything bad or mean to us. But I don't trust you to keep your promises. You promised us we'd stay all weekend. But if you weren't handcuffed right now, we'd be on our way back to that meeting."

"Steven?" Dad's voice came up the stairs. He sounded like he was trying really hard not to sound angry.

I went to the steps going downstairs. "Yeah, Dad?"

"Would you come down here for a moment?"

The thought scared me. "I don't think so."

"Are you afraid of me?"

"Yes."

"Steven, I . . . ! Have I ever hurt you?"

"Not on purpose."

"Then I don't understand."

"You're big and scary, Dad. You're a grown-up. You can yell."

"I promise I won't yell," he said.

Mom and I traded a look. She nodded, as if to say, "Why don't you go down there?"

Part of me wanted to, but I couldn't. It didn't matter what Dad promised. Speaking loud enough for both of them to hear, I said, "Look, this is a really scary thing for Benjy and me. I mean, you're our parents. You don't think we really want to keep you prisoners like this, do you?"

Neither of them answered. They were waiting to hear what else I'd say.

"We just want you to see it from our point of view," I went on. "We know you guys love us, but you never

87

have any time for us. You're always too busy with all your work things."

"Just for the moment," Mom said.

"Mom, this has to be the longest moment in history," I said. "It started when you went back to work last year and it keeps getting worse. Every time you say it's gonna end, it just gets longer."

"The trial will end," Mom said. "Soon."

"I can't imagine I'll be this busy for much longer either," Dad added.

"That's what you both say all the time," I said.

"Because it's true," Mom said.

"You said it three months ago," I reminded her.

"But things came up," Mom tried to explain. "We didn't know."

"And you don't know now either," I said. "You just *think* you know, just like you thought you knew three months ago."

Mom sighed and called down to Dad, "I think he's going to be a lawyer, James."

"We're not getting anywhere," Dad replied.

Mom turned to me. "The only phone call I really have to make is to Jack, to tell him I won't be at the meeting this afternoon."

I started toward the wall phone in the kitchen.

"But I have to speak to him, Steven." Mom held up her cell phone.

I shook my head. "I know what'll happen. You'll get off the phone and say that Jack just told you something you didn't expect. There's been some kind of new development and you're sorry, but you really, truly, and honestly have to go."

"I promise you that won't happen," Mom said.

I reached for the phone. "What's Jack's number?"

"*Steven!*" my mother snapped irritably, catching me by surprise. For a second I thought it must have been my father, but it wasn't. It was Mom. Her face was red and she grit her teeth.

"Steven, you are a twelve-year-old," she said angrily. "You have no idea what the implications of doing this are. You are behaving horribly. This is not only irresponsible, it will cause irreparable damage in innumerable ways. You have no idea the harm you're doing. I insist you release us. Right now! Or you will receive the severest punishment imaginable."

Her words felt like a hurricane-strength gale hurling straight at me. It took every bit of strength I had to stand up against them. The weird thing about words is that they *can* hurt. They can also scare. Right then I was about as scared as I'd ever been. I'd never seen Mom get mad like that before. I didn't know what to do.

"Where is the key to these handcuffs?" she demanded.

I didn't answer.

"Answer me, Steven," Mom ordered sternly.

I felt myself start to answer. I wondered if this was what being hypnotized was like. I felt like I was in her grip. "I have it."

"Come here right now and undo these handcuffs," she ordered.

I actually took a step toward her.

Mom smiled. "I knew you would do the right thing." Her voice softened. "And Steven, really, I promise . . . I absolutely swear that we'll spend more time with you and Benjy."

"When?"

"As soon as—" Mom caught herself.

"The trial is over," I finished the sentence for her.

"No, that's not what I was going to say," she said.

"Yes, it was," I said.

"For Heaven's sake, Steven," Mom blurted in frustration.

But the spell was broken. I no longer felt like I was caught in her grip. I quickly turned and headed for the door.

Down at the end of the driveway, Benjy had made a miniature corral out of pinecones, sticks, and twigs. He heard me coming and looked up. "What happened?"

"We're making progress," I said, sitting down on the rock.

"They still mad?"

"Hard to say."

"Liar," he said. "I bet they want to kill us."

I had to make more trips back to the house, but I got the feeling we were getting close to the end when Mom said she really needed to use the bathroom. I wasn't sure whether to believe her or not, but pretty soon after that she and Dad agreed to everything. They totally, absolutely swore to stay for the whole weekend and not to punish Benjy or me for making them do it. They let me take Mom's beeper, the car keys, their cell phones and laptop computers, and the kitchen wall phone, and put it all in the trunk of the car.

The car keys were a problem. If I kept them, Mom or Dad could sneak into our room that night and take them while Benjy and I were asleep. Finally I decided to put one car key on a string around my neck. I locked the car doors and threw the rest of the keys in the trunk.

"Benjy!" I stood on the deck and waved down the

driveway at my brother, who was still playing with the pinecones. "It's okay, you can come in!"

Benjy rose and brushed his hands on his jeans. I went back into the house. Mom was standing beside the fireplace with her arm stretched as far as the dog leash would allow.

"Steven, I really have to use the bathroom," she said.

"You *swear* you won't be mad at us or punish us or anything?" I asked one last time.

"Yes." She nodded. "I swear."

"And you promise not to scare Benjy or make him cry?"

"Of course."

"On your honor? Cross your heart and hope to die?"

"You really don't trust me, do you?" Mom said.

"Just promise, please?" I asked.

She nodded sadly. "I promise, hon."

I took out the handcuff key and unlocked the cuff around her wrist.

"Now I know what it's like to be held hostage." Mom rubbed her wrist, then quickly headed for the bathroom next to the kitchen.

The front door opened. Benjy stuck his head in and looked around. "Where's Mom?"

"The bathroom."

"She mad?"

"*Steven?*" Dad called up from downstairs.

"Just a second, Dad," I yelled back.

"*I thought you agreed to let us go,*" Dad said.

"I will. Just wait a second."

"You *sure* everything's okay?" Benjy asked nervously.

"It is unless they totally go back on their word," I said.

We waited until Mom came out of the bathroom. She gave Benjy a weary look.

"Remember your promise, Mom," I reminded her.

She nodded and said to Benjy, "I'm not going to be angry or punish you."

"Thanks, Mom." Benjy looked relieved.

"*Meg?*" Dad yelled from downstairs.

Mom looked surprised. "You haven't unlocked him?"

"You have to talk to him first," I said.

Mom blinked. "And get him to promise he won't get mad or punish you either?"

"Right."

She held out her hand, palm upward. I put the key to Dad's handcuffs in it. She went downstairs.

"Now what?" Benjy asked, still sounding jittery.

"We see if they really keep their promise," I said.

A moment later Mom came up from the rec room, followed by Dad. Neither of them looked happy.

"Why don't we all sit down and talk?" Mom said.

"Can we eat too?" Benjy asked. "I'm hungry."

"I'll make some sandwiches with the cold cuts," Mom said.

"And I'll just call Bill and—" Dad began, then stopped when he saw the looks Benjy and I gave him. "Oops, sorry, I forgot." He looked around. "I'll . . . I'll . . . I'm not sure *what* I'll do."

"You could have a catch with Benjy," I suggested.

"Mom, I don't want a sandwich," Benjy said. "I really want SpaghettiOs."

"Hon, we don't have SpaghettiOs," Mom replied.

"Can't you get some?" Benjy asked.

"Well . . ." Mom gazed out the big window in the kitchen. From there we could see all the way down to the bridge and the convenience store on the other side of the Bear River. "I guess we could all take a walk and see if the store has some."

That sounded pretty good. I wasn't certain we'd ever all gone for a walk together before.

"And there's a phone down there," Dad said.

Benjy and I froze. Mom rolled her eyes. "There goes *that* idea."

"I'll just go by myself," I decided.

Mom and Dad traded a wary look.

"Oh, come on," I said. "We're a million miles away from the city. Nothing's going to happen here."

Mom went to get some money. Meanwhile, Benjy had gotten his mitt. "Come on, Dad."

Benjy and Dad went outside to play ball, and I went down the road and across the bridge over the rapids. My shadow was longer now—it was afternoon, and the sun was about halfway down in the western sky. The little store was about a hundred yards away on the other side of the bridge, at the corner where you turned off the paved road and onto the gravel one that went over the bridge and up to our driveway.

I got to the store and pushed open the screen door. A little metal bell rang. I'd never been in a store like this before. The floorboards squeaked, and the air smelled musty. An old man with a wrinkled face sat on the other side of the counter. He looked up from his newspaper, nodded at me, then looked back down. I followed an aisle. The cans and boxes on the shelves were covered with a fine film of dust. It was a lot different than McKinley's in the city.

They didn't have any SpaghettiOs. I was trying to choose between a dusty can of Where's Waldo spaghetti and a dusty can of Teenaged Mutant Ninja

Turtle spaghetti when the bell on the screen door jingled again. I was sort of aware that two men had come in. Maybe it was the clunking sound of their boots. They sauntered up to the counter, bought some cigarettes, and started to talk to the old man. I didn't pay much attention until I heard one of them ask if any houses around there were for sale.

"Ain't many houses around here, period," the old man replied.

"Any sell recently?" one of the men asked.

"Just that new one across the river," the old man answered.

"Folks from around here buy it?" asked one of the men.

Something about that question made me look over the aisle at them. One was stocky with wild black hair and dark stubble covering his jaw. The other was taller and thinner. His blond hair was short, and he wore a thick bushy beard. Both were wearing tattered Army surplus jackets. They looked familiar, but I couldn't remember why.

"Bought by folks from the city, I think," the old man behind the counter said.

"No kidding?" The dark-haired one gave his friend a knowing glance. "Anything else over there?"

"What do you mean?" the old man asked.

"Any other roads?" the one with the bushy beard asked. "Any other way in or out?"

"Just this road here," said the old man. "Over the bridge to go in, over the bridge to come out."

"Okay, thanks." The men started out of the store. But at the door the dark-haired one stopped and turned back. "By the way, those folks who just bought that house, they don't drive a bright-red four-by-four, do they?"

"Nope." The old man shook his head. "Just a regular green sedan. Foreign, though."

The two men went out the door. I picked up a can of Where's Waldo spaghetti, went up to the counter, and paid.

It wasn't until I got outside and saw the two men sitting in the beat-up old red pickup truck that I remembered where I'd seen them before. That was weird. Was it a coincidence that the men I'd seen parked outside Burlington & Slater were now up here asking questions about the road we lived on?

The truck didn't move. Inside, the men were looking through the windshield, across the river, and up toward our new house. Two rifles hung on a rack behind their heads. In the back of the pickup was a big wood box with a wire door.

What were they looking at?

Why weren't they leaving?

Outside the store was a pay phone. I stopped and pretended to make a call. Standing on the porch in the deep shadow of the afternoon, I don't think the men in the truck noticed me. They were too busy looking across the river. After a while, the dark-haired one started the pickup, turned it around, and headed back down the paved road.

When I started back up the gravel road toward our house, I was determined to tell Mom about the men in the truck. But when I turned up the driveway I saw Dad out there having a catch with Benjy. It was hard to remember the last time I'd seen them do that.

"Hey, Steven, do you believe your brother's arm?" Dad asked with a smile. "I never knew he could throw that far."

Of course, he *would* have known if he'd taken time to play with Benjy, but I knew better than to say that. Instead I went into the house.

Mom was in the kitchen, mixing a pitcher of iced tea and watching Dad and Benjy through the window. She looked more relaxed and happy than I'd seen her look in months. "Did you get the SpaghettiOs?" she asked.

"They didn't have them, but I got Where's Waldo instead. Benjy won't mind."

"I hope not." Mom nodded through the window at Dad and Benjy. "Look at your brother. When have you seen him that happy?"

I looked through the window. Beyond Dad and Benjy was the gravel road, then the bridge and the convenience store. That reminded me of the two men.

"Mom, I—"

"I'm starting to think that maybe you were right," Mom said. "Maybe you did have to lock us up to get us to see how bad things had gotten. I mean, I still don't *approve* of what you did, and I'll still have hell to pay on Monday morning because I'm missing this afternoon's meeting, but seeing those two out there throwing the ball makes it *almost* worth it."

Out on the driveway, Dad threw a high pop-up. Benjy scrambled underneath it, drifting to the left, then the right, then backpedaling just like a catcher would. Only his foot hit a tree root and he lost his balance and fell backward on his butt. He lay back, stretched his arms over his head, and caught the ball. Still lying on his back, he held the ball up high like they do in the majors.

"Great catch!" Dad laughed and jogged toward him. "You okay?"

"Yeah."

Dad grabbed Benjy's hand, pulled him up, and brushed him off.

Inside the kitchen, Mom sighed wistfully. "Wonderful."

Were the two men in the pickup truck really so important? I wondered. But I knew Mom. If I told her about them she'd get upset. The magic spell would be broken.

Later we sat at the kitchen table and had either a very late lunch or an early dinner.

"Isn't this unique?" Dad asked, sitting back in his chair and looking relaxed. "No phone, no radio, no television, no newspaper, no contact at all with the outside world. It's hard to believe that people once considered this normal."

"Like the pilgrims?" Benjy asked.

"A lot more recently than that," Dad said. "It's only been the last seventy or eighty years that most people have had so many other things to do."

"Other things?" I repeated, puzzled.

"Other things than talk," Dad said. "For thousands of years people just sat around a table or a fire and talked. That was the basic form of communication. No wires, no microwaves, no satellite signals. Face-to-face. It was just about the *only* form of communication."

"Except for smoke signals," Benjy said.

"I read an article somewhere about how few families actually eat dinner together every night," Mom said. "You'd be shocked at the number."

"No, I wouldn't," I said.

Mom gave me a crooked smile. "You're right, and I know you'll never believe me, but once this trial is over, everything is going to change."

"You keep saying that, but you never tell us why," I said.

Mom leveled her gaze at Dad, and I realized that whatever the story was, he knew about it too. She turned back to Benjy and me and shook her head. "I'm sorry, kids, it's just one of those things I can't talk about."

After the meal, we played Risk. It was kind of funny. Mom was too aggressive and stretched her armies out too thin, leaving herself vulnerable to counterattack. Dad was just the opposite—he stockpiled his armies and hardly ever attacked another country. It wasn't long before Benjy and I wiped their armies off the board.

"I don't believe it," Dad sputtered. "I played as hard as I could and you *still* beat me."

"You used a really unsophisticated strategy, Dad," I said.

"The last time we played checkers I demolished you," he said.

"The last time we played checkers I was probably seven," I reminded him.

. . .

Later, Mom made popcorn and we all watched a movie together. Once during the Risk game, and again during the movie, I thought about the men in the red pickup. But it just didn't seem worth mentioning. Besides, I was having too much fun.

Then it was time for bed. Benjy wanted to sleep in my room, as usual.

"Wash up and brush your teeth," Mom said.

Benjy and I went into the bathroom and traded guilty looks.

"You remember how to brush your teeth, don't you?" I said in a low voice. Benjy nodded, then put the toothpaste on the wrong side of the brush and stuck it in his mouth.

"Exactly!" I whispered with a smile.

We went back into my room and got into the bunk bed. Mom and Dad came in together. I sort of got the feeling they'd already discussed what they were going to say.

"Boys, I have to tell you that I seriously disapprove of what you did today," Dad began.

"On the other hand," Mom added, "we see now that it may have been necessary to—uh—get our attention."

"We hope you'll never do anything like that again," Dad went on.

"We hope you'll never feel the need to," added Mom.

"We love you very much," said Dad.

Then they insisted on tucking us in and hugging us and junk. I guess that's part of life—you have to take the bad with the good.

Finally they went to the door and turned off the light. The room fell into darkness. I lay still, listening to the silence and breathing in that scent of pine.

"Steven?" Benjy whispered.

"Yeah?"

"I'm glad we did it."

"Me too," I replied in a low voice.

"What do you want to do tomorrow?"

"Don't know."

"Want to take a hike maybe?"

"Sounds good . . . No, wait. Mom forgot her comfortable shoes, remember?"

"Oh, yeah. Maybe we'll play Risk again." Benjy yawned. I heard the soft rustle of sheets and blankets and knew that he'd rolled over. He usually did that just before he fell asleep.

I lay in bed and went over the events of the day in my head. It was sort of amazing that it had actually worked. We kidnapped our own parents and held them prisoners until they agreed to our ransom demand.

Everything had gone just as I'd imagined.

Everything, that is, except . . . the men in the pickup truck.

Once again that memory crept into my mind, only this time it sat there like a big lion licking his paws and daring me to make it budge. Was it something I should have told Mom and Dad about?

But the guys in the pickup had gone away. It was probably just a coincidence that they'd been there in the first place.

Maybe I'd tell Mom and Dad and they'd just shrug it off.

Then I wouldn't have to worry about it.

Benjy's breaths were deep and steady. Knowing he was off in Never-Never Land, I slipped out of bed and left the room.

I went down the hallway. The door to my parents' room was ajar, and a thin shaft of light escaped.

I knocked. "Mom? Dad?"

"That you, Steven?" Dad said from inside.

"Yeah."

"Come in."

I pushed the door open. They were both sitting up in bed with their pajamas on, reading books. I couldn't remember the last time I'd seen them do that. And they both looked relaxed, like they weren't in a hurry to do anything else.

"What's up?" Dad asked.

"Well, uh . . ." Seeing them so comfortable made me hesitate. I didn't want to spoil it.

"Is something wrong?" Mom asked.

"I'm not sure," I said.

"You don't have to worry, hon," Mom said. "We're not angry at you anymore. I admit we were before, but we talked about it. We really do understand."

"That's not exactly what's bothering me," I said.

"What is it, Steven?" Dad asked.

"Well, it's probably nothing," I said, "but before when I went down to the store to get the Waldo spaghetti, these two guys came in and started asking questions."

"What kind of questions?" Mom's voice became calm and serious.

"Like if anyone new had bought a house around here. Stuff like that. The old guy at the store sort of described us and they asked if we drove a red four-wheel drive and he said no, a green sedan."

Dad turned to Mom. "Sounds pretty harmless, Meg."

"Yeah, except that I saw the same guys a couple of days ago parked outside Mr. Slater's store in the city," I said. "And believe me, if you saw these guys you'd know they're not into decorating."

Mom kind of gasped and let her book fall to her lap. "Fred Slater is probably the only person in the world who knows about this place."

Dad squinted at me. "Are you *sure* they were the same men?"

I nodded. "They were in this banged-up old pickup with a gun rack. They didn't have any guns outside Mr. Slater's store, but they did today."

Mom threw back the covers and started to get out of bed. "We can't take any chances, James. I want to go right now."

"Now, hold on, Meg," Dad said. "We don't know—"

"James, they were parked outside Burlington and Slater, and now they're up here asking about us," Mom said hurriedly as she pulled her jeans up under her nightgown. "Meanwhile the FBI has been warning us for weeks about the other members of the faction. Do you really think it's a coincidence?"

I sort of expected Dad to argue some more, but he didn't. Instead he threw back the covers on his side of the bed too.

"Why the FBI?" I asked. "What's a faction?"

"Go back to your room and get dressed," Mom said firmly. "Get Benjy up. This is an emergency."

Feeling a little scared, and also mad at myself for bringing it up in the first place, I went back to my room and turned on the light. Benjy was asleep with his mouth open. I shook him gently on the shoulder. "Get up, Benj."

My brother's eyes popped open. He looked around for a moment as if he wasn't certain where he was.

"Mom and Dad want us to get dressed right away," I said.

"Why?" he yawned.

"It's an emergency."

I was surprised at how fast Benjy got up and started to get dressed. "What's going on?"

"We have to leave right now," I said.

The bedroom door opened and Dad stood there tucking his pajama shirt into his pants. "Steven, where are the phones?"

"In the trunk of the car," I said.

"Give me the car keys." He held out his hand.

I gave him the key from the string around my neck. Dad frowned.

"Where are the other keys?" He asked with a tone of urgency I wasn't used to hearing.

"In the trunk with the phones," I said.

The lines in his forehead wrinkled deeply. "Is the trunk locked?"

"Yes, why?"

Dad's shoulders sagged. "Because this is the key for the rental car I use in Thailand."

Suddenly I realized what that meant. The phones were locked in the car and we couldn't get them. I'd goofed . . . big time! "I'm sorry, Dad, I—"

"Just finish getting dressed," he said sharply. "Meet us in the kitchen . . . And don't turn on any more lights."

Benjy and I were in the kitchen in no time. It was dark, but moonlight came through the windows. Mom and Dad were in the middle of a quietly heated argument.

"It's ridiculous to go sneaking out the back in the middle of the night," Dad was saying. "We walk out the front door, down the road, and over the bridge to the store. There's a phone there and we'll call."

"What if they're watching the house?" Mom asked.

"If they were watching the house, I have a feeling we'd know about it by now," said Dad.

"Maybe not," said Mom.

"Are they the other part of the faction?" I asked.

Mom and Dad looked at me, then at each other.

"What do you think they're planning to do, anyway?" Dad asked.

"These people are extremely dangerous and not terribly smart," Mom said. "I don't know what they're thinking, but I do know that all the media coverage of this trial makes me look like the leader of the government's case. They just may be thinking that if they can get rid of me they can somehow stop the whole trial."

"What do you mean, get rid of you?" Benjy asked.

Instead of answering, Mom and Dad shared another look.

"All I'm saying is that it can't hurt to go out the back and circle through the woods around the meadow," Mom said. "But whatever we do, we better do it now."

Dad nodded, and we started out the kitchen door. Then Dad stopped and went back into the kitchen. We watched silently as he opened a drawer, took out a small, sharp knife, and slipped it into his pocket.

"Just in case," he said, as if feeling the need to explain.

We left the house. The moon was out, but it was dark under the trees.

"James," Mom whispered to Dad, "let me hold on to you. I'm not very good in heels when it's flat. Here in the woods it's almost impossible."

"Would someone mind telling us what's going on?" I asked as we made our way through the dark shadows behind the house.

"Nothing," Dad replied curtly.

"Yeah, right," I grumbled. "You make us sneak out of the house in the middle of the night and nothing's going on."

"Keep your voice down," Mom said.

"But—"

"Later," she hissed. "I promise I'll explain everything."

We slowly made our way through the woods around to the side of the moonlit meadow in front of the house. Because of Mom's shoes we couldn't go very fast over the rocky ground.

"Ow!" Mom suddenly lurched sideways, pulling Dad down with her. I heard Dad grunt in pain as they both fell in the dark.

"Mom! Dad! You guys okay?" I quickly asked.

"I'm all right." Dad got to his feet. He held out his left hand and helped Mom up.

"You okay?" he whispered as she got to her feet.

"I better sit for a second." Mom's voice sounded shaky.

Dad helped her to the trunk of a fallen tree. Mom limped over and sat, then reached down and felt her ankle. "It's twisted, but not too bad. I should be able to walk."

Dad and I looked at Mom's ankle. I noticed that Dad was cradling his right hand in his left. Meanwhile, Benjy was staring back across the meadow at the house with an alarmed expression on his face. I turned to see what he was looking at.

In the moonlight, two men were stepping quietly up the front steps to the deck of our house. They were both carrying long thin things—rifles.

19

I turned to Dad, but he was already watching them. Mom, too. The looks on their faces were incredulous.

Dad cursed under his breath.

"What are they doing?" Benjy asked.

"Shush!"

The two men crossed the deck slowly. They paused beside the door. One of them propped his rifle against the wall and started to do something to the door.

"They're breaking in," Dad whispered.

"They're going to figure out we're not there," Mom whispered back.

"They'll see the car and know we couldn't have gone far," Dad whispered.

"We have to get to the store and call for help," said Mom.

"Do we all go?" Dad asked. "Or do you stay here with the boys while I go?"

Mom hadn't taken her eyes off the house. The man who'd propped his rifle against the wall was reaching through the door and inside. He must've broken the glass, but we didn't hear it.

"We all go," she said.

Dad helped her up. She went to his right side, but he told her she'd better stay on his left. We started downhill, staying in the woods beside the meadow. Mom mumbled something about her "stupid shoes." But she couldn't take them off and go barefoot. The ground was studded with sharp rocks, sticks, and pointy pine needles.

We found a trail in the woods below the meadow and made our way upstream alongside the river. It was hard to see the bridge through the trees, but we could hear the rumbling splash of the rapids beneath it.

Suddenly Dad stopped.

"What's wrong?" Mom whispered.

"The bridge." He pointed ahead. Through the tree branches we could see the dark outline of the bridge in the moonlight. I could just barely make out the form of someone standing at the railing. He brought his hand to his lips. A tiny red glow appeared.

"Think he's one of them?" I whispered.

"We can't exactly ask," Mom replied.

"We have to get to that phone," Dad said.

"Can we cross the river ourselves?" Mom asked.

We looked at the swiftly moving, swirling dark water.

"Not here," said Dad. "Maybe downstream, where they can't see us."

We followed the trail downriver until Dad stopped and told us to wait. He disappeared into the trees and came back a few moments later.

"Okay, let's try it here," he said, leading us through the dark trees. We followed him to the river's edge. Here the water moved more slowly, parting smoothly around a few big boulders poking out from the riverbed. In the dark there was no telling how deep the water was. Dad kneeled down and put his hand in.

"Cold," he muttered.

"We don't have a choice," said Mom. "We have to do it." She slipped off a shoe and put her foot in the water. When she pulled it out, I saw her grimace.

"Maybe it won't be that deep," she said.

"It'll be over our heads in the middle," Dad said solemnly.

"If it's not too far we could swim," said Mom.

"I can't," said Benjy.

Mom and Dad both turned and looked down at him.

"Can't what?" Mom asked.

"Can't swim," Benjy said.

"What about Camp Redwood?" Mom asked.

"I did computers mostly," he said.

"That camp was a fortune!" Mom fumed. "You were supposed to learn to swim this year."

"I didn't want to and they couldn't make me," Benjy said.

"I'll carry him." Dad kneeled down. "Come on, Benjy."

He climbed up on Dad's back. Dad stepped slowly into the water. After few steps the water was up to his knees. A few more steps and he was in up to his waist. I heard a sharp intake of breath. He must have been freezing.

"I'm scared." Benjy clung tightly to him.

Dad stood in the water for a moment more, then turned back. He took a step toward us and stumbled. Benjy let out a low muffled cry.

Dad's face was pale in the moonlight. "I can hardly feel my legs," he said. "You better take Benjy."

Mom limped into the water and reached toward him. Dad tried to get Benjy to let go, but my little brother clung to him.

"Easy, guy, you're not going to fall," Dad reassured him.

Benjy reluctantly let go, and Dad handed him to Mom.

I stepped into the water to help her. It was freezing! Dad came out, and we stood on the rocks and shivered. Dad's pants were soaked dark. I heard a rapid clicking sound. "What's that?"

"My teeth," Dad replied.

"Now what?" Mom asked in a low voice.

"We have to go downriver," Dad said.

"It must be twenty miles to the next bridge," Mom warned him. "They can move through the woods faster than us. They'll catch up."

"Or they'll just drive down to the next bridge and wait for us," I said.

Dad pressed his knuckles against his lips, then asked, "What's the *last* thing they expect us to do?"

"Go back to the house?" Benjy guessed.

"If we could get the phone in the car trunk . . ." Mom mused.

Dad shook his head. "Not without making an awful lot of noise. What if I distract the one on the bridge? Maybe he'll come after me and you three can get across."

"Unless he figures out what you're up to," Mom said. "Then all you'll do is let him know where we are."

"Maybe," Dad said. "But I can't think of anything else, can you?"

No one spoke. The river drifted past slowly, making lapping sounds.

119

"We could cross the bridge," Benjy suggested.

"He'll see us," Dad said.

"Not if we climb under it," said my brother. "Like on all that metal stuff."

"If you fall it's right into the rapids," Mom said.

Ruff! In the distance a dog barked.

Ruff! Ruff! Then another.

"Oh, hell!" Dad whispered hoarsely. "They've got dogs!"

Mom quickly looked back at the river. "We have to cross here."

"Not a chance," Dad said. "Come on." He reached for Mom's arm and started to lead her along the riverbank.

"Where?" Mom asked.

"The bridge," Dad said. "We have to try Benjy's idea."

With Dad helping Mom, we hurried along the riverbank. The bridge loomed up ahead in the moonlight. As we went toward it, we were met by the muffled roar of the rapids. The air grew damp with a cold mist. We couldn't see the man who'd been smoking the cigarette.

"Do you think he left?" Mom asked.

Dad shook his head. "They know the bridge is our only way out. He's up there somewhere."

Mom hesitated. "Then won't he see us?"

"I hope not," Dad said. "We're in the shadows of the trees. And with those rapids, he sure can't hear us."

The bridge was close now. Still helping Mom, Dad moved steadily toward it. I'd never seen him act like this before, like he was completely in charge. We stopped at the edge of the tree shadows. Between here and the beginning of the bridge was fifty feet of riverbank dimly lit by the moon.

"Now what?" Mom whispered.

"We go quickly and quietly and hope they don't see us," Dad whispered back. He turned to Benjy and me. "Ready?"

Benjy shook his head. His eyes were wide with fear. "What if they see us?"

Mom and Dad shared a look. Then Mom kneeled down and took my brother's hands in hers. "You're not the one they want. No matter what happens, you have to find a way to the other side. No matter what, understand?"

Benjy nodded slowly and wiped a tear from his eye.

"You have to be brave, hon," Mom told him. Then she turned to me. "You too, Steven. You have to help your brother."

I nodded, but I was so scared I was shaking.

"Okay, we better do it," Dad said, reaching for Mom's hand.

"Wait!" Mom pulled her hand back. She was staring up at the bridge. We all looked up.

A man was up there, staring back down at us.

No one moved or spoke or even took a breath. The man on the bridge couldn't have been more than twenty-five yards away. It seemed like he looked right at us, but his face revealed nothing. We watched, frozen, as he reached into his shirt pocket and pulled out a cigarette, then cupped his hands and lit it. The ember glowed red. He exhaled a long plume of smoke and turned away.

"He didn't see us." Dad sounded almost giddy. "Now come on. Let's go before he comes back."

With Mom hobbling as fast as she could, we hurried across the loose dirt and rocks beside the raging rapids. A moment later we'd made it! We ducked into the shadows under the bridge and caught our breaths.

It was almost pitch black under the bridge. My brother and parents were dark shapes. The air was cold, and as misty as fog. The roar of the rapids echoed in our ears. I pressed my back against the concrete base and felt the cold dampness seep through my jacket.

Stretching up above us were dozens of crisscrossing girders spanning the bottom of the bridge. They were crusted with dirt and rust. The mist collected on them and dripped off.

Dad pointed up at them, and Benjy nodded. Mom looked grim.

But it was our only chance.

Dad helped Benjy up first. My brother grabbed the lowest girder and pulled himself over it, then shimmied on his stomach toward the next.

I went next, grabbing the first girder. Some of the crusty dirt came off under my grip. The metal was cold and wet. Dad gave me a boost and I climbed up over it, then spread out over the next two.

Then Dad helped Mom. She grabbed the girder while he pushed from below and I pulled from above. Wincing and grunting, Mom managed to climb up. Now it was Dad's turn.

"Come on, Dad," Benjy hissed down to him.

Dad shook his head. "You help Mom get over to the other side. I'll go back into the woods and lead them away."

"James, no!" Mom pleaded.

"You have to come with us, Dad," I said.

He held up his right hand. It was thick and swollen. "I can't. I hurt my hand before."

"You have to *try,*" Benjy urged him.

"The dogs," Mom reminded him.

Dad grabbed the girder and tried to pull himself up. He could hold on with his left hand, but his right was pretty useless. After a moment he gave up.

"Go on." He cradled his right hand in his left again. "I'll wait here."

"No way." I reached down toward him.

"I can't, Steven," Dad said.

"Just try," I pleaded.

Dad grabbed the girder again. This time I reached down and held his right arm around the elbow. Benjy crawled over and managed to snag the bottom of Dad's pants leg.

"Whoa!" The weight of Dad's leg started to pull him off the girder. "Mom!"

Mom grabbed Benjy.

"Let go," Dad said, afraid that he'd drag us all down.

"Forget it." I kept my grip on his elbow. Benjy stopped sliding. Mom was holding him. I started to pull his elbow. "Come on, Dad!"

Dad heaved himself a little higher, then grimaced in pain. "I can't . . ."

I could feel him starting to slip back down. "You have to do it."

He gathered himself, and with one final effort made it up.

"Okay, hold it," I said.

Dad was breathing hard. "Not . . . like . . . I . . . have . . . a . . . lot . . . of . . . choice," he panted. "Is it okay . . . if I just rest for a moment?"

"Sure."

Dad closed his left hand over mine. "I never thought I'd make it . . . Thanks, Steven."

"No sweat, Dad." I felt a smile spread across my face.

We waited for him to catch his breath. Below us, the fast-moving rapids roared over the rocks. Somewhere above, men with rifles and dogs were hunting for us.

When Dad was ready, we started to climb across the girders, banging and scraping our knees and elbows on the cold, dirty metal. Still, the farther we got from shore, the better I felt.

Until I realized that the space between the girders and the roadway above us was slowly narrowing. Ahead of us, Benjy stopped. Then me. Then Mom and

Dad. We all stared ahead at the place where the girders met the bottom of the roadway, leaving no space to crawl through.

No one said a word. I watched Mom and Dad share a look, silently raising the question with their eyes of what to do next. We were stuck in the middle of the night, clinging to girders under a bridge. Forty feet below us the torrent of water smashed through the jagged rapids.

"We could wait," Dad suggested. "Sooner or later someone has to come looking for us."

"What happens when the sun comes up?" I asked.

Dad didn't answer.

"They'll see us," Mom said. "We're sitting ducks here. We have to go back."

"No," Dad argued. "We don't stand a chance back there."

"We don't stand a chance *here*," Mom replied sharply.

The waters below us roared. The cold wet mist chilled us to the bone.

"Hey, guys!" Benjy called.

I looked around. For a second it seemed like he'd vanished.

"Over here!" He was off to the side, near the metalwork along the side of the bridge.

"Benjy!" Mom gasped. "Come back here."

"No, I can do it," Benjy said. "I can get across."

He wanted to crawl along the metalwork to the other side. It would mean going hand over hand with his legs dangling below, but it was the only way to get past the middle part of the bridge.

"No!" Mom said.

"I could go with him," I offered.

"It's out of the question," Mom insisted.

"What would you do if you got across?" Dad asked.

"The phone at the store," I said. "We could call for help."

"Are you sure you can make it?" Dad asked Benjy.

"Sure," he said. "It's just like at home."

"No, it's not," Mom said. "It's wet and slippery and you've never done it before. I won't let you go alone."

"Why not?" I asked. "You always left us alone at home."

The waters roared.

"That was different," Mom said.

Groof! Ruff!

The dogs were on the riverbank.

Next to the bridge.

G *roof! Ruff!*
Through the murky darkness I could barely make
out the creatures moving excitedly up and down the
riverbank. Then I heard another sound—the crunch
of heavy boots on loose rock.

"Think they tried to get across here?" a man's
voice came out of the mist and dark, yelling over the
roar.

"Through the rapids?" Another voice laughed. "If
they did they just made our job a whole lot easier."

"You think?"

"Maybe, maybe not. Let's keep goin' upstream.
Maybe they went that way. Spark! Dynamite! Let's
go!"

The men and their dogs headed upstream along the
riverbank. I turned back to Mom and Dad.

"Benjy and I can do it," I said. "We've done it hundreds of times."

"Thousands," Benjy added.

"I can't allow it," Mom said stubbornly.

The rapids crashed and boiled forty feet below. I looked at Dad. This was our only chance. In his face I could see that he knew it.

I turned to Benjy. "Go on. I'll be right behind you."

"No!" Mom's voice rose anxiously.

"Yes," I said.

"James, stop them," Mom pleaded.

"It's our only chance," Dad said.

Benjy grabbed the bottom of the I-shaped girder and swung off into the air. A second later he was dangling over the river.

"Oh my God!" Mom gave a muffled groan.

My brother began to go hand over hand toward the other side. I started to follow.

"Wait, Steven." Dad stretched toward me with something in his left hand. It was his wallet. "My telephone calling card's in it. Dial zero, then the area code and phone number, then the number on the—"

"I know how to use a calling card, Dad."

He scowled in the dark. "How?"

"This is modern times," I replied. "*Every* twelve-year-old knows."

"He doesn't need a calling card, for Pete's sake." Mom sounded aggravated. "He's going to dial 911."

"Take it just in case," Dad said.

I took it, then made sure I had a good grip on the I-shaped girder and swung out into the air.

23

A few minutes later we dropped down to the riverbed on the other side of the bridge. It felt good to be on solid ground again. We quickly made our way up the riverbank. A ditch ran alongside the gravel road. It was lined with tall grass, and the bottom was dry. Benjy and I crouched in it and looked back at the bridge. At the other end a red ember glowed. The cigarette guy was smoking again.

"Head for the store," I whispered to Benjy.

Staying low, we scampered along the ditch until we reached the store. No lights were on inside. The moon had moved to the western part of the sky, and I knew it was later than Benjy or I had ever been up before. Just how late was hard to tell.

Benjy and I slipped around the side of the store. The

pay phone was on the front porch in the moon's shadow.

"I'll make the call," I whispered. "You watch the bridge in case any of those guys—" I stopped and stared at the phone.

"What's wrong?" my brother asked.

"Look."

Benjy looked at the phone and frowned. "What *is* that?"

"A dial," I said. I stuck my finger in it, spun in, and let go.

"Does it work?" Benjy asked.

I picked up the receiver and heard a dial tone. With Benjy keeping an eye out for the bad guys, I dialed 911. It rang for a long time. Then a sleepy-sounding woman's voice answered. "Yeah?"

"This is an emergency!" I whispered anxiously. "We need help! These guys are after us!"

"Who is this?" the voice sounded more awake now.

"My name's Steven Marks," I said.

"Who?"

I repeated my name and explained about our new weekend house.

"Where are you calling from?"

"A store."

"Where?"

"Near the bridge on the Bear River."

"The Bear River is three hundred miles long. You're going to have to do better than that."

"But I don't know where . . ."

"You in Jefferson County? Spring Glade?"

"I don't know," I said. "This is our first time here. My mom and dad are hiding under the bridge. These guys with dogs and guns are looking for them."

"Why?"

"My Mom's doing this trial," I explained. "She's the chief prosecutor. They think if they get her it'll stop the trial."

"Not that Freedom Militia thing?" the woman asked.

"Yes!" I gasped. "That's it!"

"Gee, I was just watching that the other day on TV," she said. "What's your mom's name?"

"Megan Marks," I said.

"Yup, that's right. Short black hair, used to wear the same dress all the time, then she got a whole new wardrobe. Guess everyone goes Hollywood sooner or later."

"She's not going to Hollywood or anyplace else if we don't get help quick," I said. "This is serious!"

"Steven!" Benjy tugged on my shirt.

I put my hand over the receiver. "What?"

My brother pointed. In the moonlight I could see two men with rifles walking along the bridge toward us.

I put the phone to my ear. "Hello?" No one answered. The line was dead.

Benjy and I backed around the corner of the convenience store. Even in the dark I could see that my brother's eyes were wide with fright. But he couldn't have been any more scared than me.

We were separated from Mom and Dad.

The bad guys were coming.

Benjy and I were just defenseless kids.

"Jeez, I can't believe you, Carl," one of the men said. As they came closer, Benjy and I backed farther around the convenience store.

"Hey, man, I just didn't think of it," Carl replied.

"You didn't think we could use a flashlight while huntin' around in the dark for those fools?"

"Sorry, Trav."

"*Sorry, Trav,*" Trav repeated in a high-pitched, mocking tone. "How many you got?"

"Just the one, but it's nine-volt."

They were close now. Benjy and I pressed ourselves against the outside of the store.

Screak! It was the door to the pickup truck opening.

"Here you go," Carl said.

I heard a soft click. "Darn, that's good!" The man named Trav chuckled.

"Told you it was nine-volt," Carl replied proudly.

"Yeah, if only you'd told me two hours ago," Trav muttered. "Who the heck knows where they are now?"

Bang! The pickup's door slammed shut.

"You sweating, Steven?" Benjy whispered beside me.

I wiped my hand across my forehead and felt the cold, frightened perspiration that had gathered there. "Yeah."

"Me too."

"Congratulations." I peeked around the corner again. Carl and Trav were walking back across the bridge, the beam of the flashlight bouncing along the roadbed ahead of them.

"We have to go back," Benjy said in a low voice.

"Why?" I asked.

"I don't want to leave Mom and Dad there."

"Neither do I," I replied. "But the last thing they want us to do is come back."

"We have to," Benjy insisted. "Otherwise the bad guys are gonna find them with the flashlight."

He was probably right, but I was scared. As long as we were on the store side of the bridge, we had a chance to escape. Once we got back under the bridge, we were sitting ducks again . . . Just like Mom and Dad were at that very second.

"Okay," I said. "But if we're going back, let's at least take something with us so we can help them get across."

Benjy pointed to a curled-up garden hose hanging on the convenience-store wall. "What about this?"

It was worth a try. I unscrewed the hose from the spigot and draped it over my shoulder.

By now the bad guys were back on the far side of the bridge. They had stopped to talk to the cigarette smoker. The man with the flashlight swept the beam through the trees and along the riverbank.

As Benjy and I started back toward the bridge, I saw the beam of the flashlight way up on the other side of the road near our house. The bad guys had gone back to the house again. Maybe they thought we were hiding inside in a place they hadn't noticed before.

Then I realized something important. The bad guys

didn't know where *we* were, but as long as they had that flashlight, we'd know where *they* were.

"Why did you come back?" Mom asked angrily when we climbed back under the bridge to them.

"Benjy said we had to," I explained. "He didn't want to leave you here. Besides, they have a flashlight now."

"We saw it," Dad said. "What happened with the phone?"

I told him about calling 911, but not knowing where we were.

"Did you try anyone else?" Dad asked. "What about the calling card?"

"It was an old phone with a dial," I said. "It didn't have any buttons."

"All you had to do was call an operator," Dad said.

"Oh." I felt stupid. "I didn't know."

"It's okay," Mom said. "You boys have been fabulous. And so brave."

"Now we can all go back across," Benjy said. "With the hose."

Mom and Dad looked at each other in the dark.

"You go," Dad said to her.

"Not without you."

"Go," Dad urged her. "You're the one they want.

I'm useless to them. Even if they get me, it won't stop the trial."

"We'll all go," Benjy said. "One at a time."

"I can't." Dad shook his head. "My hand's shot. I can't even bend the fingers anymore."

Ruff! Groof!

"It's the dogs!" Benjy cried. Down the riverbank, we saw the flashlight beam coming toward us. Suddenly it rose up and swept across the bridge, flashing in our eyes.

"He just checked the bridge," Mom whispered.

"What do we do?" I asked.

"Nothing," Dad whispered back. "Just hold on and pray they don't see us."

The men came upstream toward the bridge.

Ruff! Ruff! The dogs barked and tugged at their leashes.

The flashlight beam swept the riverbank and trees. Every so often it would angle off against the far riverbank or up at the bridge, where it would send a chill of terror down our spines.

Dad, Mom, Benjy, and I tucked ourselves up as close to the dark cold underneath of the bridge as we could. Despite my fear, I suddenly had to yawn. A wave of fatigue washed through me.

"I'm scared," Benjy whimpered.

"Shhhh!" Dad whispered gently. "We don't want the dogs to hear us."

The flashlight beam grew brighter as it came closer, sweeping the rocky riverbank.

Groof! Groof! Ruff! Ruff! The dogs were making a racket.

Beneath us the rushing waters roared.

The men and dogs reached the bridge and stopped near the concrete base.

"Dang, I don't get it," the one called Trav said loudly over the rapids. "This is the second time the dogs led us back here. They get under this darn bridge and they don't want to leave."

The beam of the flashlight swept up the girders under the bridge, casting light and shadows against the underside of the roadway.

Groof! Groof! Groof! The barks grew louder and more insistent.

I pressed my cheek against a cold wet girder and held my breath. My heart pounded, and I felt the blood throbbing in my forehead. Were they going to see us?

Grooof! Grooof!

The flashlight beam zagged away.

"Will you shut them dogs up!" Trav snapped.

"What do you want me to do, Trav?" Carl asked. "Shoot 'em?"

"You shoot a dog and I'll shoot you," Trav answered.

Groof! Groof! Groof!

"Know what I bet they did? Heard the dogs and decided to wade upstream to throw 'em off the scent."

"But we been up that way already," Carl said.

"Maybe not far enough," Trav said. "Not that they could get far in this ice water. Let's go upriver again. Sooner or later they had to climb out. The dogs'll pick up the scent where they did."

Groof! Groof! Groof!

They started upstream, the flashlight beam sweeping the riverbank ahead of them.

A wave of relief swept through us.

"That was too close," Mom moaned. "I thought my heart was going to stop."

"You three have to get out of here now," Dad said firmly.

"No," said Mom.

"Listen," Dad said, "they won't go upstream forever. Sooner or later they'll wind up back here again. And look"—he held up his wristwatch. It had one of those dials that lights up— "it's almost five-thirty. Another half an hour and it'll start to get light out."

Dad spoke softly and steadily about why we had to leave him. We didn't stand a chance once the sun came up. He wasn't the one they wanted anyway. We had to save ourselves.

"So what if something happens to me?" he said. "I'm never around anyway."

"Don't say that," I said.

"When you're not home we look forward to seeing you," Benjy said. "If we knew you weren't coming back it would be totally different."

"Well, if and when we get out of this mess, I guarantee you I'll be around a lot more," Dad promised.

"Hey, don't strain your credibility, Dad," I said.

He actually smiled a little. "Go on, you better go."

"You have to come with us," Mom said. "You have to try."

"It's no good, sweetheart. I can't do it." Dad held up his right hand. In the slowly growing light it looked really swollen. "I think it's broken. I'm better off hiding. Now go. I'm serious. You're running out of time."

In the dark I thought I saw Mom's eyes start to glisten with tears. Then I heard her sniff. Dad reached out with his left hand and squeezed her arm. "Not now, sweetheart. Remember the kids."

Mom turned to Benjy and me. "Lead the way, boys."

I held up the hose. "Let's set it up for her."

"Right."

Using the knife Dad had taken from the kitchen, we

cut the hose in half. Holding one end in his teeth, Benjy hand-walked to the other side of the bridge.

"How am I going to do that?" Mom whispered as we watched him.

"Just slide your hands along," I said, making a harness around her waist with the other end of the hose. "You don't have to go hand over hand like Benjy. He's just showing off."

"What do I do?" she asked.

"Grab hold of the edge with both hands and slowly let yourself hang. It's better if you don't look down."

Mom gazed quietly at me.

"What is it?" I asked.

"It's hard to believe how much you've grown up," she said. "I keep wondering how it happened. Especially since I had almost nothing to do with it."

"Maybe it wouldn't have happened otherwise," I said.

"Do you hate me?" she asked.

I looked up at her in surprise. "What are you talking about?"

"For being such a lousy mother," she said.

"No way."

"I told you it was all going to change after the trial," Mom said. "And it will."

I nodded. By now Benjy had tied his end of the hose

to the other side of the bridge. If Mom lost her grip, the hose would stop her from falling.

"Ready to go?" I asked her.

Mom didn't budge. "I mean it, Steven."

"I know you do, Mom, but—"

"There'll be a book," she said.

"What?"

"I'm going to write a book about the trial," she explained. "But it's an absolute secret. You can't tell a soul. If the media ever found out it could hurt the trial."

"Okay," I said.

"It means I'll be home," she went on. "I'll write the book at home. I'll be there to make breakfast and dinner and to see that you brush your teeth."

"Why are you telling me this now?" I asked.

Mom looked down at the rapids and back at me. "Because if anything happens, I want you to know that I really intended to keep my word."

I just stared at her in the dark. Maybe I was grown up, but I still felt like crawling into her arms and being hugged. Maybe that's a need you never lose, even when you get old. Only we didn't have time for that now.

Mom took hold of the bottom of the I-shaped girder, then hesitated and looked down at the roiling waters.

"Don't look down," I reminded her.

"You might as well tell me not to imagine a big pink elephant," she quipped.

"Just let yourself hang," I said. "We've tied the hose tight. If you can't hold on, the harness will hold you."

I held on to the hose while Mom slowly let herself down under the I-shaped girder.

"Can you do it?" I asked.

"Do I have a choice?" She started to work her way toward the middle of the bridge. The hose went tight. Out of the corner of my eye I looked upstream. There was no sign of the men or the flashlight beam. But the sky to the east was beginning to lose the darkness. The stars were starting to disappear.

The hose loosened. Mom had made it to the other side.

"How's she doing?" Dad whispered from behind me.

"Okay, I think."

"There's not much time," Dad said. "I'm proud of you, son."

"You're a lot braver than I thought, Dad," I said.

He smiled a little. "Well, there's a backhanded compliment, if I've ever heard one."

"I meant that I didn't know before," I said.

He nodded. "I guess fathers don't get a lot of opportunities to prove it one way or the other these days."

"You did," I said.

He nodded. "Get going."

Then I grabbed on to the I-shaped girder and swung out under the bridge.

It was growing lighter. By the time Mom, Benjy, and I reached the far side of the bridge, the sky in the east no longer resembled night at all, but the deep blue-gray of early dawn. We dropped to the ground and quickly started up the riverbank. Where before it was too dark to see the other side of the river, we could see it now.

We reached the ditch beside the road and followed it to the convenience store. Mom limped to the phone. The shade of the porch didn't offer much protection now, so Benjy and I stayed around the side of the store while Mom pressed herself against the wall and dialed 911.

The sky was turning gray.

We waited.

"What's going on?" I whispered.

"No one's answering," Mom replied, her face twisted with concern.

Ruff! Ruff! In the distance we could hear the dogs barking.

"Oh, come on, answer already!" Mom muttered anxiously.

She kept the phone pressed to her ear.

Groof! Ruff! The barking was louder and closer.

"They're gonna see us," I hissed. "Or the dogs'll smell us or something."

Mom's eyes darted quickly around.

"The truck," she whispered, letting go of the phone. She left it hanging and limped quickly toward the pickup. Benjy and I followed.

The windows were open. Mom stuck her head in. "The key's in it. Come on."

Benjy and I climbed in the passenger side. Mom got in on the driver's side. The floor and dashboard were littered with empty plastic cups, cigarettes butts, and dog hair.

Benjy wrinkled his nose. "Wow, it really smells in here."

Mom reached for the key and turned it. The truck started. She stared down at the floor. "Oh, no! It's a manual!"

"So?"

"I only know how to drive an automatic," Mom said.

"I can do it," I said.

She gave me an astonished look. "You know how to drive?"

I nodded.

She didn't doubt me for a second. "The next thing I know, you'll tell me you know Chinese." She got out and started around to the passenger side of the pickup. I slid over behind the wheel.

Meanwhile, Benjy stared at me. "What are you doing?"

"Driving, what else?" I said.

"You don't know how."

"Max Horsepower, man."

"That's a video game."

"Same thing." I gripped the steering wheel. "Here's the wheel, there's the gas, and there's the gearshift. It's even got the same shift diagram. First, second, third, fourth."

Mom got in the passenger side and pulled the door closed.

I pressed down on the gas, grabbed the gearshift, and pushed it toward first gear.

Screeeeech! The pickup made a high-pitched grinding sound and didn't move.

"*That's* not like the video game," Benjy said.

Mom looked anxious. "I thought you said you knew how to drive."

"A video game," Benjy said.

"Oh, Lord!" Mom pushed open the passenger door and hobbled around to the driver's side again. "Move over." She pulled open the door and slid back in behind the wheel. "What was I thinking?" she muttered, staring down at the controls.

"Uh-oh!" Benjy cried. "Look!"

Mom and I both looked up. The guy on the bridge was running toward us.

Mom quickly looked down under the dashboard at the pedals. "What do I do? What do I do?" She started pressing the pedals. The engine roared when she hit the gas. Nothing happened when she hit the pedal next to it. When she pressed on the pedal next to that, it went in.

"I know what that is!" Mom said excitedly. "The clutch!"

She pressed it in, then jammed the gearshift forward.

"But, Mom, that's—" I started to say.

Mom let the clutch out. The truck suddenly lurched forward, snapping our necks back, then stalled.

"—fourth gear," I finished.

"Hey!" The man from the bridge had reached the gravel road on our side. He was running hard.

Mom turned the key again and the engine roared

back to life. She pushed in the clutch and grabbed the gearshift again.

"Try number one," I said, closing my hands over hers and helping her push the shift forward.

Mom let out the clutch. Again the pickup lurched, but this time it rolled a few feet before it sputtered and stalled.

"Mom!" Benjy screamed. The man was only a few dozen feet away now.

"Lock the door and roll up the window!" Mom shouted as she turned the key. I reached across Benjy and jammed the door lock down, then started to crank the window up.

Varroom! The engine roared to life.

Slam! The man banged into the side of the truck and managed to get his arm partway in before I got the window all the way up. He got me by the hair and pulled.

"Ow!" I screamed in pain. "Mom!"

The truck lurched forward again and started to roll. The man held on to my hair and started to run alongside the truck.

"Ow! Ow! Ow!" I screamed in pain.

"Do something, Benjy!" Mom shouted.

Benjy grabbed the window crank and tried to turn it. Meanwhile, the truck's engine roared as Mom floored it and we started to go faster.

"Ow! Ow!" It felt like he was pulling my hair out.

Benjy kept pushing on the crank, squeezing the man's arm.

The truck's engine whined.

"Uhn!" With a grunt, the man let go.

I straightened up. My scalp throbbed.

Benjy grinned proudly.

The truck's engine roared so loud it sounded like it was going to explode.

"Why won't this darn thing go any faster?" Mom asked, staring down at the gearshift.

"It's the gears," I said. "You have to push it into a higher gear."

"How?"

"The same way you pushed it into that one," I said.

"But what if . . . Ahhhh!" Mom suddenly screamed. The guy was on her side now!

Mom's window was down. The guy held on to the door frame with his right hand and reached in with his left, trying to get the keys to turn off the ignition. Mom was holding the wheel with one hand and hitting his arm with the other.

But given the fact that Mom's fist was about the size of a tennis ball, she didn't seem to be making much of an impact.

The pickup veered and skidded as Mom tried to steer with the guy hanging to the side. Mom kept hitting him. Somehow she managed to steer the truck off the gravel road and onto the blacktop highway.

"You gotta shift, Mom!" I shouted.

"How?" Mom screamed back.

"With your hand," I yelled. "Into second gear!"

"I can't with *him* hanging on!"

We were weaving and skidding frantically down the road. Every time the guy's hand came near the keys we'd knock it away. Meanwhile the pickup's engine whined as Mom kept it floored in first gear. White smoke was pouring out the tailpipe, and the warning lights on the dashboard were glowing red.

In the confusion I suddenly realized that the guy's hand had disappeared. He was still holding on to the door frame with his right. I stretched up and craned my neck to look over Mom and see what he was doing.

With his left hand, he was trying to pull a knife out of a leather sheath!

"He's getting a knife, Mom!" I yelled.

"Oh, God!" Mom's jaw dropped. For a split second she just stared at the man's right hand, the one he was holding on to the door with. Then in one swift movement, she reached down toward her feet and came up with one of those black shoes with the pointy heel.

Whack! She slammed the heel down as hard as she could right on the man's knuckles. I heard a cry, and the pickup shook. He let go!

Benjy and I twisted around. Out the back window we saw him tumbling on the road behind us.

We both turned and stared at Mom in awe. She was

hunched behind the wheel, her eyes narrowed and her jaw set with determination. One hand was on the wheel. In the other she still held the shoe.

"I *knew* they'd come in handy for *something*," she said, and dropped the shoe to the floor.

30

About half a mile down the road, the pickup's engine blew with a huge burst of white smoke. Mom jammed on the brakes. In the distance we could see the flashing red lights of a police car coming toward us.

"Cool move, Mom," I said.

"Yeah," Benjy agreed.

"It was an act of desperation," Mom replied without taking her eyes off the approaching police car. "Otherwise, I don't advocate violence as a solution to anything."

Benjy and I stared at her in disbelief.

"Geez, Mom," my brother finally said, "lighten up already."

Mom grinned a little. The police car was coming closer. We got out of the truck and started to wave.

It turned out that the 911 dispatcher had sent police cars all up and down the Bear River, looking for a convenience store near a bridge.

We told the officer in the car what had happened and that Dad was under the bridge. He radioed for backup help, then put on his siren and drove up toward the store. We found out later that he caught the man with the knife and arrested him, then waited at the bridge for more police cars to arrive.

Benjy and I wanted to run back up the road toward the bridge, but Mom wouldn't let us because the bad guys had rifles and, well, you never know what they might do. We had some tense moments until the rest of the police cars arrived and we heard that Dad was okay under the bridge. The bad guys never saw him.

Mom's trial ended about three weeks later. The Nut Bombers were convicted of stockpiling bombs for use against the government and for possessing illegal assault weapons. Mom said they were going away for a long time.

"What about the guys who tried to get us?" I asked at breakfast the morning after the trial ended.

"They're going away for a long time, too," Mom replied as she dumped some pancake mix into a bowl and cracked in a few eggs.

"Is that why the police aren't in front of our house anymore and we don't need Mr. Sam to take us to school?" I asked.

"That's right," Mom said.

"Can't we get Mr. Sam back?" Benjy sounded cranky. "I don't like walking all the way to school."

"Tough," Mom replied with a big smile as she poured some milk into the bowl.

"What's for breakfast?" Dad asked as he came into the kitchen, wearing his business clothes. He'd just gotten back from his latest trip to Thailand a few days before.

"I'm making the boys pancakes," Mom said. "But there's melon and cottage cheese in the fridge."

"Oh, uh, good." Dad didn't seem really excited. "You know, I could use something a little more filling this morning. I think I'll have pancakes and save the melon for tomorrow."

Mom gave him a stern look. Dad smiled sheepishly and poured himself a mug of coffee.

Benjy looked up at the clock. "You don't have time for pancakes, Dad. You're late for work."

"No, I'm not," Dad said. "If I have to spend half my life on the other side of the world, I can take time to have breakfast with my family when I'm on *this* side of the world."

Ding Dong! The doorbell rang.

Groof! Groof! Pearson bounded out of the kitchen.

"Who's that?" Benjy asked.

Before Mom could answer, the front door opened.

"Down, furball!" Dewey's voice carried in from the front hall. A moment later he came into the kitchen.

163

"Hey, you're getting seriously domestic," he said.

"I thought you were leaving this morning," Mom said.

"I am," Dewey answered. "Just stopped in to say good-bye."

"Where're you going?" Benjy asked.

"Into the heartland, Benjo," Dewey said. "Gonna do your Mom's grunt work."

Benjy scowled and looked at Mom, who was pouring pancake batter into a pan on the stove. "What's he talking about?"

"I need a research assistant," Mom explained. "If I'm going to write a book about the Nut Bombers, I need to know something about their backgrounds and childhoods. I've hired Dewey to go to their hometowns and talk to people who knew them growing up."

"We're gonna dig down deep into the twisted root of terrorism," Dewey said with a grin.

"Just make sure you take lots of notes and get as much as you can on tape," Mom reminded him.

"Piece of cake, Mrs. Marks." Dewey lifted an invisible microphone to his lips. "This is Dewey Van DeHey, investigative researcher/reporter, on the go and on the job."

He gave us a wave and left the kitchen. As soon as

he was gone, Dad gave Mom a concerned look. "Are you sure he's the best one for the job?"

"It's worth a try," Mom said with a shrug. "Think about the kind of people the Nut Bombers grew up with. Do you think they'd be more willing to talk to a slick city lady like me, or to a guy like Dewey?"

Dad nodded. "You've got a point."

"You bet I do." Mom crunched up some Oreos in a soup bowl. "Want your pancakes with Oreos or without?"

"Without," Dad said.

Mom only added the Oreo chunks to the pancakes for Benjy and me.

A few minutes later they were ready.

"Hey!" Benjy took a bite and sat up straight. "These are perfect! The Oreo chunks aren't soggy. How come none of our nannies could make them like this?"

"Probably because they always mixed the chunks in the batter too early," Mom said. "They got soggy."

"Why didn't you tell them not to?" Benjy asked.

Mom smiled. "Maybe I didn't want them to make it as well as I do."

"Huh?" Benjy didn't get it.

"She didn't want us to forget who our real mother was," I explained.

"That's right," Mom said. "And now your real

mother is going to tell you both to finish your milk and make sure you brush your teeth before you go to school this morning."

"Aw, Mom, do we *have* to?" Benjy whined.

"Hey," Mom said with a smile, "no complaining. You wanted your real mother. Now you got her."

About the Author

Todd Strasser has written many award-winning novels for young and teenage readers. Among his best-known books are *Help! I'm Trapped in Obedience School* and *Girl Gives Birth to Own Prom Date*. He speaks frequently at schools about the craft of writing and conducts writing workshops for young people. He and his family live outside New York City with their yellow Labrador retriever, Mac.